Contents

A Note from the Author

This book contains explicit content, including graphic sex: DP, knotting, butt play (penetration with a vibrating gargoyle tail), the exchange of blood, cursing, a beheading, violence, and a kidnapping. Discussions of a verbally abusive marriage that impacted the FMC's confidence in her appearance, minor mention of weight (when the FMC is talking about her ex), weight loss (side character), and a mention of cheating (not by main character).

This book also includes scenes discussing mental health and visiting a psychiatric hospital (FMC's mother), an age gap relationship (MMC's 999, FMC's 40), fated mates, and instaLUST.

If you have concerns, or a specific trigger, please reach out to the author.

Help is available

Suicide & Crisis Lifeline — Call or Text: 988

https://988lifeline.org/

https://afsp.org/

https://nami.org/Home

National Domestic Violence Hotline: 800-799-7233 or

Text START to 88788

https://www.thehotline.org/

Please consider donating to St. Jude:

https://www.stjude.org/

Playlist

The Beginning of the End – Klergy, Valerie Broussard
Black Cathedral – This Cold Night
In the Shadows – Amy Stroup
For Whom The Bell Tolls (Remastered) – Metallica
Monster – Lady Gaga
In the Air Tonight – Jon Howard
Another Way Out – Hollywood Undead
Gods & Monsters – Lana Del Rey
Fate – H.E.R.
I Believe in a Thing Called Love – The Darkness

Listen to the playlist here:

Vibrating Tail.

That's it.

That's the dedication.

Chapter 1 - Evangeline

Fuck. I need to get laid.

I set my vibrator down. The toy did its job, getting me off. It's one of those dildos with a thrusting feature and an extended piece that massages the clit.

I came, and it was good.

So why do I feel so empty? So...unsatisfied?

I need to be dicked. I need to be fucked so hard, my cunt is sore for days. I've never had good sex like that, especially with my ex-husband, who is the only man I've ever slept with.

My phone dings on the bedside table, reminding me it's time to get ready for work. I am *not* looking forward to this shift. Last night, from the moment I clocked in at seven p.m., it was non-stop patients. I didn't even sit down and eat until I got home at eight in the morning.

At least the night goes by fast when I'm busy. I don't have to think about my life's failures. I mean, sure, I have a decent job. I'm a night nurse in New York City making enough money to afford a cute one-bedroom apartment in NoLita.

But I'm not happy. I haven't been for a while.

I'm a divorcée, and my ex-husband treated me like shit. He weaponized my height and weight. I'm five foot one and 250 pounds. He criticized what he considered my lack of dreams—I don't want to be a doctor. I love being a nurse; I just want to care for people in need when they're at their weakest. He made me believe I wasn't worthy every damn day until something clicked, and I realized *he* was wrong, and *he* was the one who wasn't worthy of *me*.

It's been six months since our divorce was finalized, but our marriage had been dead for years before that. Working to build myself back up from his verbal abuse has been exhausting.

It's also been rewarding because for the first time in my life, I'm getting to know myself. I'm discovering what I like and what I hate, without anyone telling me what I *should* like or *should* hate.

Now, I'm more than ready to move on. I'm ready to start dating again, but fuck, I'm terrified. Mostly because, how do I go about it? Do I go to a bar? That's something I did in my twenties, and I wasn't even on the market then. Going to bars at age forty while single? I think I'd rather yeet myself into the ocean while on my period and make friends with hungry sharks. See, that's another thing. Yeet? Are people my age allowed to say words like that? What if I go to a bar and blurt out slang that's no longer 'in'? Yeah, no bars. I'd feel too out of place.

I could hang out in the produce section of the grocery store. Maybe find me a date who can cook me dinner—and breakfast, if it's a good enough date. I'm a horrible cook. I can make scrambled eggs and pancakes, a simple pasta dish or a kickass salad, burgers are easy enough, and chili is my specialty dish. Beyond that, I'm clueless.

Wait. No. Cooking dinner for someone is such an intimate thing to do. Staying the night and having them make breakfast the next morning screams second date, which potentially leads to a third date, then commitment, and I'm not looking to be tied down to another man.

I'm not looking for a soulmate.

As if those even exist.

God, I sound so bitter. I blame my ex for that. Maybe I should just download a dating app since I'm wanting more of a hookup right now.

I pick up my phone and groan. The apps and my shitty dating life will have to wait until tomorrow morning because I'm about to be late.

My shower is quick since I don't wash my hair, which is something I do once every couple of days. I pick out a fresh pair of scrubs from my laundry basket—I hate putting away clothes. After pinning my thick, wavy brown hair into a tight bun at the top of my head, I give my adorable black cat Birdie—because her meow sounds more like a chirping bird—a kiss on the head and leave.

The hospital I work at is a few blocks away. Walking there should only take five minutes, but sometimes I get distracted by the buildings and stop to admire the stunning structures, especially the Basilica of St. Patrick's Old Cathedral. I discovered the church a few weeks ago after taking a different route to work. I'm not religious at all, but there's something about the building that's...familiar. Comforting.

Sometimes, after a rough shift at work, and once the parish opens at 8:30 a.m., I'll go inside and sit in the pews, closing my eyes and listening. The silence is heavy yet healing.

The gothic architecture is hauntingly beautiful. My eyes are always drawn to the highest point of the building...as if something is up there, waiting for me. It doesn't scare me. It's intriguing, tempting almost.

The church is closed when I go into work, and if I wouldn't get arrested for trespassing, I'd hop the fence and go find what's silently calling to me.

Tonight, the church's pull is nearly too strong to avoid. It's...painful as I walk away. My stomach twists, and nausea washes over me. But I can't stay tonight. I can't linger and stare into the void like I do some evenings because I'm already late for my shift.

When I get to work, my coworkers are running around. The chaos has already started: gunshot victims, people with chest pain, people who were hit by falling debris from a building—literally my worst fear. Actually, my apartment catching fire is my worst fear because I will die trying to save my cat instead of myself.

Speaking of fires, halfway through my shift, we get a call about a massive blaze at a nearby high-rise. Dozens of patients are heading our way to be treated for smoke inhalation, burns, or injuries sustained while trying to escape in a panic.

I barely have time to breathe by the time my shift ends. The only thing I ate was a granola bar I keep in my scrubs pocket for nights like tonight, and I didn't sit down once, unless sitting on the toilet to pee counts.

When I leave work, the sun is out. It's summer, and the morning is warm. I bask in the golden rays and the slight breeze that smells like the bakery on my block. I consider stopping for an apple cinnamon muffin or a cream-filled donut, but I'm trying not to spend any unnecessary money. New York City is expensive and moving here drained me of my savings.

Once home, I make myself a bowl of cereal and sit on the couch watching the morning news, tuning out the details of the apartment fire. Most of the patients I treated tonight told me everything I needed to know: hearing the alarms, seeing the smoke filling the hallways, running down thirty floors of stairs to safety.

Not everyone made it out alive.

My phone beeps with a notification, and I open it to find a red bubble hovering over a new app.

Kis-meet.

A dating app? Huh. That's weird. I didn't download this. At least, I don't think I did. Wait. Did I do it before going to work? The night was so chaotic, it's possible I downloaded it and forgot.

I open the app, and it takes me to a screen to fill out my details.

Okay. I guess this is happening.

Name: Eva

No. Brandon called me Eva. Since moving to Manhattan, I've been introducing myself as Evangeline. I left Eva in Upstate New York.

Age: 40

I cringe when entering that number. I never thought I'd be on a fucking dating app at my age. Oh well, maybe I'll meet someone my age. Or a silver fox in his sixties. Or some hot twenty-something-year-old who wants to date a plus-size cougar.

Height: 5'1"
Eye Color: Blue
Hair Color: Brown
Location: Manhattan

I hit submit, and it takes me to a screen to upload a picture. I choose a recent one that shows off my body. I know men can be weird about fat women. Most want to fuck us but not date us. Right now, I'm okay with that. Like I said, I'm not looking for commitment. Still, I put a whole-body photo so they can't be surprised that I'm a big girl.

The picture is from my first day after moving here a few months ago. I accepted the nursing job and left the small town where I grew up in Upstate New York. I had to leave. I couldn't stand being in the same town as my ex-husband anymore, even though I had long moved out of the home we shared and lived in a studio apartment I could barely afford on my school nurse salary.

I'm smiling in this photo. I asked a stranger to take it while visiting the Top of the Rock. It was the first time in years I felt *happy.* My chipmunk cheeks are dimpled, and my blue eyes light up with something other than sadness and defeat. I'm wearing a purple spaghetti strap sundress, which shows off the floral tattoos along my arms, shoulders, and chest.

The tattoos consist of white heather flowers, which symbolize protection. I also have purple Evangeline lilacs because ever since I was a kid, I've been obsessed with the flower that I share a name with. My mother told me Evangeline means the bearer of good news. She said I was her rainbow baby. She always worried something was going to take me away from her.

Not some*one.* Some*thing.*

She'd keep white heathers around my crib and throughout the house for protection. As I grew older, she'd tell me stories about supernatural beings who lived among us. Beings that could be evil. Beings that wanted to harm me. She'd stuff my backpack with the flowers before I left the house for school and made sure I wore the heather bracelet and necklace she made me—pieces of jewelry that Brandon threw away one day, thinking they were trash.

I was furious at him, which prompted me to get the tattoos the next day. He hated them, but I didn't care. The tattoos weren't for him or me. They were for my mother who'd been begging me to get them since I turned eighteen.

Me marking my body with ink might have been the moment Brandon fell out of love with me. We'd fight constantly after that, especially if it involved my mother.

He hated that I kept her in my life.

I was ten years old when my father found out she believed an evil being wanted to kidnap me. He sent her away to a psychiatric hospital where she remains today. I try to visit her once a week, but she doesn't talk much anymore. Sometimes, I go just to sit with her, or read to her, or let her know I still love her.

I haven't seen her in months, ever since I moved to the city and work a busy job. I don't have a car anymore either and the train ride to the hospital would take at least two hours because the town isn't along a main line.

Birdie jumps into my lap and jolts me out of my thoughts. She rubs her face against mine and chirps, letting me know it's time to eat.

"Okay, Birdie Girl. Let me finish this, and I'll get your breakfast."

I take one more look at the photo. My hair is styled perfectly around my face in waves. I gave myself bangs and a wolf cut a year ago, and now I'm obsessed. I've always liked the clothes and style of the seventies and eighties, and now I have the hair to match.

"Here goes nothing," I say and tap submit.

The app processes and takes me to an empty page, where I assume my matches will be displayed. I search for the section where I can swipe or heart profiles, but I must be exhausted, because it's nowhere to be found. My brain is struggling to function.

Okay. I'll figure that out when I wake up this evening. I exit *Kis-meet* and set my phone on the table.

After feeding Birdie and showering the night away, I crawl into bed and fall asleep dreaming about a sexy man, tall and packed full of muscles with...lavender skin?

Chapter 2 - Xander

The night is quiet. Too quiet.

I've been protecting New York City for over four hundred years now, ever since Dutch settlers arrived in 1608 and named the land New Amsterdam. Before ruling my own kingdom, I patrolled the skies over Paris under my father's reign. He taught me everything about fighting the evil that yearns to destroy the world: the demons from hell and the malevolent creatures from other worlds who slip through the cracks between dimensions.

The Council of Gargoyle Elders chose me over my older brother as king of this new settlement, which seers had envisioned becoming one of the largest cities in the world.

They were right.

I watched as New Amsterdam transformed into a bustling city with humans in the millions. Too many innocent souls wandering the streets needing protection. As New York City grew, so did my army. I have gargoyles in the thousands now, spread around the five boroughs. They're stationed on top of buildings, keeping watch for any attempts to pierce through our shields of protection.

The shields have become weak as I approach my thousandth year of living. I have six months until I permanently turn to stone.

The life of King Xander the Third of New Amsterdam, his excellency of house Basque, son of King Oberon Basque of Lutetia Parisiorum, now modern-day Paris, comes to an end, all because he couldn't find love.

I would become the second king in my kind's history to die because I failed to find my fated mate.

It's a curse of every royal. We are stronger with our soulmate by our side. I've spent hundreds of years in search of the one who claims my heart. I've held extravagant balls and invited men and women from across the world. I've courted thousands of beings, both human and supernatural, in hopes that they were my fated mate.

Yet I am still alone, and my kingdom is in peril. Evil lingers, waiting for me to fail.

"Your Majesty," Locheran, my first in command says, approaching me from behind.

It's a busy Friday night. I stand on the roof of the Basilica of St. Patrick's Old Cathedral, staring below at the crowds of people strolling down the sidewalk. Laughter and chatter fill the air from nearby bars and restaurants. The streets are packed with cars unnecessarily honking their horns.

"You've been standing here for hours. Do you sense an attack?"

I exhale and rub my hand up and down my face.

"No."

It's all I say because I can't tell my closest advisor that I felt a pull in my chest again tonight. He worries about me, concerned that the curse will soon shut down my body, my organs, and I will no longer be able to rule.

I have six months left. I will fight until the very end.

The pull in my chest started a few weeks ago. I was in my penthouse when it felt as if someone was ripping my heart out. It lasted minutes, if that. I blamed the pain on the curse, until it happened again the next night, but the sun hadn't fully set yet, so I wasn't able to emerge to investigate.

The sun temporarily turns gargoyles to stone, and we're left vulnerable until night falls. It's a damnation placed on our kind centuries ago after panic spread through a small village in Europe when a child saw a gargoyle flying through the sky while protecting the land. The frantic child's family went to a witch who knew all about our existence. She knew we were there to keep evil away, but to satisfy the humans, she sentenced us to the night when mortals sleep.

Of course, times are different now and the world stays awake at all hours. Because of this, we've developed the ability to mask our true forms.

The problem with not being able to go out in the sun means cities are left unguarded during the day. While we have shields in place, they're weaker in the sun. Evil beings tend to be nocturnal; however, there are a rare few who can walk during the day.

It's been decades since the last time we faced a threat. An army of soul-sucking demons from another realm attempted to break through our barriers. The stench of innocent human souls lured them out of the depths of whatever hell they derived from. It was a battle that lasted all through the night until the sun rose and turned some of my soldiers to stone.

Another threat is on the horizon. I feel it in my bones.

The evil infused within this world knows…it senses the end of my reign.

"We should go to the bars. Find you someone to fuck. Your stress is weighing us all down," Locheran says.

Being the king means all the gargoyles within my kingdom are connected to me. They experience my emotions, my pain.

Thankfully, they don't experience my pleasure, only emotions that alert them to me being in danger. It allows them to locate me and come to my side to protect me from whatever is trying to cause me harm.

My stress must be taxing on my body enough to be felt amongst them.

"The bars are useless. My fated mate would not frequent one of those vile breeding grounds. It's all sex, sex, sex, and I can get that with the snap of my finger—"

"Aren't you a confident motherfucker—"

"Fuck off, Loch."

He chuckles, the asshole. Locheran has been my advisor since the moment I was crowned king, but we've known each other since we were young pups. We're best friends, and we joined my father's army together. We've killed evil side-by-side. We're inseparable. Yet he doesn't face the same fate as me. He can turn one thousand and not have to worry about permanently turning to stone.

He's yet to find his fated mate, though many gargoyles don't. For royals, it's imperative that we do. Only one other king failed to find his soulmate. When he turned to stone, his replacement had not yet arrived, and the city was burned to the ground by a fire-breathing demon. A fire that killed thousands and was blamed on a human's mistake.

"I will stand guard here until the sun wakes," I say. "You go. Enjoy yourself. We'll meet tomorrow night to go over reports."

Locheran sighs dramatically and walks away without saying a word.

The rest of the night went by without incident, thankfully, because my thoughts were too focused on the pull in my chest and the possible cause. I've traced it to the cathedral, and that's why I've been sleeping here lately. The moment night falls, I emerge to the cathedral's roof to find the source of the connection, only for it to be severed.

That's the only way to describe it. A connection. A cord tying me to something.

Or someone.

I fly home to my penthouse down the street from the Basilica. The building has roof access so I can enter as my true form instead of shapeshifting into a human, which has been draining me of energy lately.

God, why is everything fucked?

My eyes are struggling to stay open, but I know the moment my head hits the pillow, my worries will keep me awake.

I shower and jack off, trying to relieve some of my tension. I'd much prefer a cunt, asshole, or mouth around my cock, but fucking for fun is less desirable when you're six months away from a lifetime of stone.

So, I take my pleasure by hand.

Once I'm done, I dress in a t-shirt and sweats, then collapse onto the couch and turn on the television to a local news program. A reporter is talking about a deadly fire at a nearby high-rise apartment. My soldiers informed me of the blaze. I sent them in to investigate, but there was nothing supernatural about it.

I know they're restless. They sense the threat as well. We're on edge, waiting for our shields to be penetrated.

My phone dings with a notification, and I unlock it, thinking it will be a drunken text from Locheran. Instead, I find a new app on the home screen.

Kis-meet.

Did that fucker download a dating app on my phone?

To be fair, we've yet to resort to dating apps. We've embraced the technological advances of this world, but dating apps? I've resisted, because why would my fated mate be on one of these so-called hookup apps?

Why wouldn't they be?

Fuck it. What do I have to lose other than my life?

I tap the screen, and it takes me to a page to enter my details. Is this an app for humans or paranormal beings? I play it safe and enter the details for my human form.

Name: Xander

Age: 30

Height: 6'4"

Eye Color: Blue

Hair Color: Black

Location: Manhattan

I tap submit, and it takes me to a page to upload a photo. I select one where my skin isn't purple, and I have no horns, fangs, mane of blue hair, silver eyes, or flapping tail.

After it uploads, my page is live, and I go back to give it a once-over.

"What the fuck?" I repeatedly poke my finger at the screen, trying to delete the photo, because that's *not* what I uploaded.

Did I select the wrong one? The photo on display is of my true form—snapped by Locheran a few years ago on a drunken night. Well, he was drunk. I was his DF—Designated Flyer. I rarely get wasted anymore. It takes too much alcohol in my body to do anything of worth. I let my soldiers party, and I watch over them because they deserve to be rewarded for their hard work protecting this city.

I try to change the photo back to one of my human form, but it automatically reverts to this casual image of the real me. Seriously? Could this weird app at least choose one where I'm in battle gear, or in a suit for fuck's sake?

My age and height also do not reflect my human form.

Age: 999

Height: 7'

Before I can fix this mess, I get a notification.

One match?

How?

I just signed up! I didn't even do the swiping or liking or whatever dating apps require.

I stare at the notification for a few minutes before opening it. I'm too curious to ignore how strange this is.

> ***You've matched with Evangeline. Human, 40, Manhattan.***

A human? Not many know about us. Perhaps this is one of those exclusive dating apps that pairs paranormals with humans. Why else would it specify that she's human?

This one is quite beautiful. She has a button nose, and her round cheeks dimple when she smiles. She's five foot one, with blue eyes and brown hair that feathers around her face and bangs. She has beautiful floral tattoos along her arms, shoulders, and chest. Her body is full and round in the most pleasant way.

My cock agrees, hardening despite me draining it of cum just minutes ago.

Evangeline.

The name means divine protector in my world.

Could this be another gargoyle? No. I know every gargoyle in the city. Besides, she's clearly human. Though, I did try to upload a human photo myself and the app changed it. I have no clue if this picture is of her true form.

I select the option to message her.

What do I say? Will she even respond? Maybe I should let her message me first.

No, I'm too eager to know more about this woman. Just her name and her beautiful face call to me. Her luscious body has my cock begging to be deep inside her cunt.

God, I sound like a fucking asshole. A sex fiend. I'm never like this.

Which is why I need to meet her immediately.

Me

Hello Queen

No. That's coming off a little too strong. Delete.

Hello Evangeline. You're my first match on this app. I have to say I'm blown away by your beauty.

Bleck. No. Delete.

Get it together, Xander. Don't scare her away. I look at her details again. She's five foot one. I'm seven feet.

Fuck, she's tiny.

I'm going to destroy her.

I stand up and pace the living room. What the fuck am I going to say? I open Google and search opening lines for dating apps.

There are some good ones, but for the most part, they're cheesy as hell. I wish this damn app would have let us fill out more information about ourselves. At least then, I could read some of her interests and work from there.

God, what the fuck kind of dating app is this?

Okay. Let's just...be honest. Be...real.

I've been trying to figure out what to say in my first message to you. I'm really bad at this. Dating apps seem so impersonal which is why I've never used them before. I'm pretty sure my friend downloaded this one on my phone because I don't remember doing it my-

> **self. I suppose I should thank him though as I've matched with you. You're stunning.**

I hit send and blow out a long stream of breath.

Okay. That wasn't hard. I kept it casual. Real. I didn't care about grammar or punctuation. Not that I've ever been good with that shit, but I've learned in these modern times that text messages tend to be informal.

Wait. Should I ask her a question? Did I ramble too much? I suppose I don't need to add more nonsense.

Wow. 999 years of my life, and I still get nervous when meeting a beautiful being. Except, I've never felt this on edge with any other potential lover.

I set my phone down, deciding to let fate take the wheel. I can't imagine what she's going to think the moment she sees a gargoyle has messaged her.

Chapter 3 - Evangeline

My alarm jolts me awake, and I pick up my phone, prepared to throw it across the room. Ugh. Why the hell did I set my alarm? It's Saturday and my day off.

Birdie jumps on my chest and starts making biscuits, her claws digging into my skin through the thin fabric of my sleep shirt.

"Okay! I'm up, I'm up!"

She jumps down, and I throw the covers off my body, then drag my ass to the bathroom to relieve myself and brush my teeth.

I feed Birdie her dinner, make myself coffee, and toss two frozen waffles into the toaster. Once my sad little breakfast is nice and crispy, I slather it with butter and syrup and sit on a stool at the counter to dig in.

My phone beeps with notifications. I start with texts, first answering my father to assure him I haven't been mugged or murdered.

Next, I respond to my bestie, Farrah, asking about plans for my birthday in August, which is still a couple months away. I'd love to do a singles cruise this year. Farrah is my age and swears after too many failed relationships that she'll never get married.

She still lives upstate in Macedon and teaches at the same school where I worked as a nurse before moving to NYC. She gives me all the gossip about my ex and other assholes in that town who I no longer care about—but love hearing the tea on.

My boss also texted me, asking if I'd pick up an extra shift next week, which I agree to, since I could always use a bigger paycheck.

I skim through my emails but don't see anything pressing. I'm about to go to my social media accounts, where I never post but mostly lurk and doom scroll, when I spot a red bubble hovering over the *Kis-meet* app.

My heart kicks into gear and pounds against my chest.

Did I get a match? How? I didn't even swipe or heart any profiles.

My finger shakes as I tap the icon. Why am I so nervous? Maybe it's because I'm forty years old on a dating app.

You have 1 new message.

A message? Holy shit. Okay. It's fine. You can do this.

I open it, holding my breath.

Xander

> **I've been trying to figure out what to say in my first message to you. I'm really bad at thls. Dating apps seem so impersonal which is why I've never used them before. I'm pretty sure my friend downloaded this one on my phone because I don't remember doing it my-self. I suppose I should thank him though as I've matched with you. You're stunning.**

I smile.

He thinks I'm stunning.

I don't let the compliment get to my head, because Far-rah—who's been bullying me into getting on the dating apps—warned me about love bombing.

I tap on Xander's profile and burst out laughing.

What the hell? He has horns and fangs and... lavender skin.

Just like in my dream.

Suddenly, it all makes sense.

I'm losing my mind, because surely this can't be real. Am I still asleep? A dream within a dream? Dreamception?

I look at Xander's photo again. I mean…he's fucking hot. He's not wearing a shirt and abs ripple up and down his torso. His meaty chest and cords of muscle along his arms and shoulders are like art. His *hair*. It's dark blue and disappears down his back. His eyes are *silver,* and his fangy smile could light up a room.

He has *horns*. I can't help imagining myself clutching them while I ride his…

My eyes trail down to his sweats and the massive bulge.

If this is a cosplay costume, it's one of the best I've seen. *If?*

I mean, it has to be cosplay, right? The horns, fangs, tail, and wings…but if it's cosplay, why would he be wearing sweats? Why not warrior's gear or even a suit? This is clearly a candid someone took of him.

If… because I always believed those stories my mother told me about supernatural beings who lived in the shadows and blended in with humans. I pretended I didn't believe her because she asked me to keep it a secret.

Our little secret.

All my life hearing her stories about the supernatural, yet I've never met one. Could Xander be my first? I'm going into this with an open mind.

I add a kissy face and hit send.

Wait.

Did I really just say "let's be bad together?"

That's opening myself up for an unsolicited dick pic.

Though, if he really is a supernatural being, he might not have a human-like penis. Would it be ribbed for my pleasure? Would he have TWO?

Okay. Wow. I'm horny.

My phone chirps with a response, and my face flushes, my heart could bruise my chest with how fast it beats as I read his reply.

Me

Why can't we do both?

Xander

Both?

Me

Yeah. Have dinner then be bad.

God, what is wrong with me? This man...this *being*...has me acting feral.

Xander

Evangeline...I do not think you know what you're insinuating.

Me

I know exactly what I'm insinuating.

Xander

Ok. I'll play. You want to be bad? Fuck the small talk. Let's meet. Tonight at 8. Mulberry Street in front of old St. Patrick's Cathedral.

Me

A church? Are we going to sin and ask for forgiveness after?

Okay, now I'm being *naughty*.

If you don't stop being a brat then you'll definitely be on your knees praying for penance.

Oh, fuck.

And it won't be God's name you're calling.

Holy shit.

My nipples are painfully hard, my panties soaked as his words paint pictures in my head: Him fucking my mouth. Him taking me from behind. Me *begging* to come.

See you at 8 bad boy.

I add a winky face emoji and close out of the app, too scared to see his response. I'm also freaking out just a little bit.

I've never sexted someone before. My ex wasn't into it. Not that my texts to Xander could even qualify as sexting. They were rather tame, but boy was it exhilarating.

I'm also nervous because I've never had a one-night stand. People do it all the time, so why can't I?

I've only slept with one man: my ex, Brandon. I met him as a freshman in high school, and we began dating the next year. We talked about splitting up after graduation, but our colleges were only an hour apart, so we stayed together.

Brandon doesn't like change. He had a life plan: get his law degree, get married, land a job at a firm. He got everything he wanted.

We were married for fifteen miserable years. Well, not all of those fifteen years were horrible. He was a decent husband for our first five years of marriage, then he slowly lost interest. I'm pretty sure he cheated on me with his secretary.

He fought me on the divorce. He didn't want it, claiming it would make him look bad amongst his colleagues. I didn't care. I served him papers a week later. He made sure to punish me for leaving him too. He knew all the loopholes to get everything in the divorce. All I got was Birdie, but she was all I needed.

Fuck that asshole.

I wasted too much time on him. I never got a chance to live.

Now it's my turn to be careless and free. I deserve this. Tonight, I'm going to fuck a stranger. I'm going to let him *destroy* me.

I wonder if Xander uses that tail during sex?

I check the time. Nearly six. I have two hours to prepare my body.

Shower. Shave—everything. Lotion.

I keep my makeup simple, choosing cherry lip gloss and brown eyeshadow for a light smokey eye. I style my hair to feather around my face.

The summer night is hot, so the red dress I choose is short, with spaghetti straps to show off my tattoos. It also has built in support, which I don't need a lot of since I'm a member of the itty-bitty-titty committee. I look sexy as hell in this dress, and I hope I won't be wearing it long.

With one more look in the mirror, I slip on my black heels and grab my clutch.

The walk takes less than five minutes since I live close to the landmark cathedral. The moment the metal fence surrounding the building comes into view, my heart beats faster.

I become lightheaded, which always happens when I'm near this church. The dizziness doesn't last long, only when I'm in this area. I never really thought about that being strange until tonight.

I'm too anxious to dwell on that thought though.

I arrive at the gate, but it's locked. Sweat gathers on my lower back and at the nape of my neck.

Yep. I'm nervous. God, I hope I don't look a mess. At least I smell good. Before I left, I sprayed myself with one of my favorite perfumes, which has hints of strawberries and marshmallows.

I turn in circles, looking for my lavender man.

"Um, Xander?" I say out loud.

"I'm here," a voice from behind says, making me jump.

I whip around, ready to throw punches, and find Xander standing an arm's length away, his eyebrows furrowed.

I tilt my head to see him. And I mean all of him, to the tip of his horns. His wings may be tucked to his back, but they're unmistakably there. His tail whips back and forth behind him.

"So it's not cosplay," I whisper.

His pinched forehead grows deeper, and he frowns. "I don't understand."

"You have horns and wings and a tail. What are you?"

He takes a step back and shakes his head.

"You shouldn't be able to see my true form. I masked myself. I..."

When I move closer to him, he freezes hauntingly still. Like a statue. God, he's beautiful. And he smells fantastic, like leather and bergamot. He's dressed in all black, a tunic and dress pants. It's casual yet stylish and slightly old-fashioned.

I reach up my hand and place my palm on his chest in the middle of the v of the shirt. His skin burns underneath my touch, but I don't pull it away. He's smooth, like stone…or marble. But it's not hard nor cold. I want to run my hands all over his body, and I'm not sure why. Almost as if the moment we made eye contact, waves of euphoria were shot throughout my body.

Does he feel the same?

"What are you?" I ask again, my voice soft and low and in awe of this being before me.

"I'm a gargoyle," he growls and grabs my neck, squeezing hard enough to make me yelp.

Instead of being scared, I'm turned on, and I whimper as he tightens his hold.

"My question, Evangeline, is what are *you?*"

Chapter 4 - Xander

She's divine.

An angel.

Or she's evil, here to tempt me.

"Tell me," I say and back her up against the metal fence. Fuck, I wish she'd stop whimpering. It's confusing my cock, which wants nothing more than to sink into her cunt in this moment.

She's stunning, even more so than her picture on the app. Her curves are plentiful. That red dress does nothing to hide them from me. I can hear her heart beating frantically, her breathing heavy. Her pale skin is blushed pink, and my eyes fall to the tattoos lining her arms, shoulders, and chest. Evangeline lilacs mixed with ones I recognize as heathers because they're a symbol of protection, just as her name means divine protector in my world.

The coincidence doesn't get past me, but I'll revisit this later, as I need to know how the fuck can she see my true form.

"Xander," she whispers, her voice strained from my grip around her neck. Yet, I cannot smell her fear. I see no panic on her face. No, all she's giving me is lust and excitement. "My name is Evangeline Bishop-Whethers. I'm human."

I loosen my grip slightly because she's right. Everything about her is weak. Well, weak only because she is human. I have no idea how strong of a human she could be.

I also sense no magic within her except for the hum of power radiating from her tattoos. A protection spell. Why would she need a protection spell?

Now's not the time to ask her that question.

My paranoia has clouded my judgment. I let my fear of evil convince me this woman is here to kill me. She may not be supernatural, but she's different from all the other humans I've encountered throughout my years.

I release her neck and sniff in her direction, trying to figure out why she's special. My cock strains against my pants. It likes this sweet smell on her body.

I need more. I grab her hair to tilt back her head and run my nose along her skin. I inhale deeply, and she gasps and arches her back to press her soft body against mine.

"Did you just growl?" she asks, sounding amused.

I let go of her hair and step back.

"Did I?"

"Yeah," she smiles and bites her lip. "It sounded like this..."

She proceeds to make a noise that is anything but a growl. It was like a kitten attempting a frightening roar.

It was freaking adorable.

"I could kill you with my bare hands and you're mocking me?"

She giggles. "Sorry, I'm not mocking, I swear. This is just surreal. I've never met a supernatural being before."

"You know about us?"

"Well, yes and no. My mom used to tell me stories. She said there were bad beings and good ones. I think you're a good one."

I suck in a sharp breath.

"You're not afraid of me?"

She shakes her head.

"Why?"

"I can't explain why, but I know you won't hurt me. Scared is the last thing I'm feeling right now."

I raise a brow, and she smiles; her cheeks darkening with a lovely red to match her pouty lips.

"What *are* you feeling right now?" I ask.

She's most definitely aroused. I can smell how wet she is, which doesn't help my erection.

"By the way your nostrils just flared, I think you already know."

I open my mouth then clamp it shut. Her eyes trail down my body to my groin where she can see how turned on I am.

"Then we should do something about it," I say and close the distance between us.

I wrap my arm around her waist and tug her body against mine. She's incredibly short, and the top of her head barely reaches my chest.

"Do you trust me?"

"Should I? Are gargoyles trustworthy? Plus...we just met. It'd be pretty dumb of me to trust someone I've known for mere minutes."

She looks up at me, fluttering her long, full lashes and licks her lips.

"You're teasing me."

"Maybe I am."

I lean in, my mouth against her ear. "Are you being a little brat?"

"What if I am? What would you do about it?"

I chuckle, and she shivers as my hot breath fans across the exposed skin of her neck.

"Naughty kitten," I whisper, only because her beauty and defiance have captured my voice. She leaves me speechless, and I have so much to say to her right now.

I have too much to ask her.

But we're in public, and I'm currently masking us from the human world. I need my full focus on her.

I need to fly us out of here.

"I'll ask you again, Kitten. Do you trust me?"

Her pupils expand at the nickname. She likes it. Good.

"I trust you, Xander."

I nearly groan at how my name sounds in her smooth, honey voice.

"Hold on tight," I say and catapult us into the night sky.

Evangeline screams and buries her face in my chest, nearly choking me with how tight her arms are around my neck. Her thick legs flail before wrapping around my waist.

"I've got you," I say as we hover over the city. My expansive wings flap slowly to keep us steady.

Her body relaxes slightly at my words, but she still clings to me tightly. Hesitantly, she removes her face from its hiding spot and opens one eye...then another.

"Holy shit," she gasps. Her big blue eyes scan the skyline. "This is...beautiful."

Tonight, the Empire State Building sparkles in bright purple and pink colors. Skyscraper windows light up in a checkerboard pattern with a handful of late-night workers. Inside the high-rise apartments, windows glow from televisions playing TV shows or movies. Evangeline glances below us at the sea of red and white from the heavy traffic on New York City streets.

She immediately buries her head back in my chest.

"I'm not a fan of heights," she mumbles into my shirt.

"Tell me where you want to go."

I hope she doesn't say home, unless she invites me inside too. There's no way I'm letting her go without asking her all the questions plaguing my thoughts.

"Take me to your place," she says.

I smile, and her eyes fall to my fangs. Shit! I didn't mean to have those out. They tend to drop when I'm turned on. I immediately close my mouth.

"No, don't." Her hand moves to my lips, and she traces her fingertips over them lightly. I sigh at how *delicate* she is with me. As if *I* will break underneath her touch. "Can I feel them?"

I hesitate only for a second, stunned by her curiosity...then exhilarated that she wants to explore me.

I smile for her again.

Her tiny finger swipes over one long fang, down to the tip, where she presses the pad into the sharp end. The scent of iron fills my nose. She pulls her hand back and slips the pricked finger inside her mouth to suck the blood. I swallow my jealousy.

I wanted a taste. Would her blood be as sweet as her smell?

Fuck. I'm in trouble.

This woman is going to ruin me.

"You did it again."

"What?"

"You growled."

"I'm a beast. I growl all the time."

Not entirely true. I growl when I'm threatened...or when I'm aroused. And now that I know this woman is no threat to me, my reaction to her is pure, unadulterated passion. My attraction to this woman is nothing humane. It's intense, and I can't explain it.

More questions I need answered.

"I like it. Maybe a little too much. I might try to make you growl all the time now."

She moves her hips, her legs still wrapped tight around me. Her pussy rubs against my bulge and that gets her another growl.

"That's what Kitten wants to hear," she purrs.

She's adopted the nickname already? She's too good to be true.

"Take me to your place," she repeats breathlessly, reminding me that we can't stay up in the air all night.

She'll need to get over her fear of heights, because I'd love to give her a mid-air fuck after I've properly bedded her.

Chapter 5 - Evangeline

I'm acting like a cat in heat.

But the way he called me a naughty kitten? It was sexy as hell!

I'm definitely being naughty.

My overactive hormones seem to be overshadowing my fear of heights. I feel safe in Xander's arms. His words and nearness calm me in a way I can't explain. It made me forget we were hundreds of feet in the air. Or would it be dozens of feet? I don't even know, but the longer we hover, my body flush with his, the more my fear transforms into *excitement*.

Xander flies us a few blocks away to a high-rise. He must be rich. This building is full of luxury units. I remember seeing a listing for a unit when I was apartment hunting that was three times more than what I pay for rent. My building is an old, pre-war walk-up with appliances that haven't been updated in the last twenty years. At least I live close enough to work that I can walk.

We land on the roof—smoother than a plane landing on a runway—and I attempt to dismount the gargoyle, but he tightens his arms around me.

"I can walk now."

"I know," he chuckles, and the deep, hearty sound vibrates throughout my body.

"I'm too heavy. Just let me walk."

"Does it look like I'm straining? Can you see me sweating?"

My hands mindlessly run up and down his muscular arms. They're massive. Okay, fine. I suppose he's got that supernatural strength going for him.

"Convinced?" He raises his brow—perfectly sculptured like the rest of his body.

I realize I'm still petting him and squeezing his muscles. I can't help it. His skin has such a unique texture. It's soft despite appearing hard, and it's coated with fur-like hair.

"Sorry, I've never been carried around before."

"Ever?"

"Not as an adult, no."

I've been fat my whole life. There are things I've never experienced like being picked up by a man and carried around as if I weigh nothing. Things I've been limited to because I was either too self-conscious (like wearing crop tops out in public), or because my body wouldn't allow it (like being comfortable on airplanes or amusement park rides).

These things used to bother me. I let the world tell me I wasn't worthy, and then my ex-husband's verbal abuse solidified those views. It wasn't until my fortieth birthday last year, when Farrah and I took a train into New York City to celebrate, that everything changed.

I wore a skintight dress. I put on make-up and cut my hair and dyed the grays away. For once, I cared about my appearance—instead of letting Brandon convince me I wasn't hot enough to care—and I looked fucking amazing.

That night, I had men hitting on me left and right. And even though I wasn't at a point to let them take me home, I still felt beautiful. That's when I realized my whole life had been a lie. It was never about how the world viewed me, but how I viewed myself.

"Evangeline." Xander's deep voice startles me, and I jolt in his arms. "Where did you go?"

"Sorry," I whisper.

He walks us into an elevator and pushes a button. The doors close, and he presses my back against the wall, then reaches up and clutches my chin between his fingers.

"Never be sorry."

I smile.

"What if I do something that deserves an apology?"

He leans in and rubs his nose up and down my cheek.

"Then you atone."

He presses his velvet soft lips to my neck, and I gasp when he sucks and laps his tongue over the skin.

"Is this okay?"

"Yes, sir." The words come out in rasp.

"Sir?"

I can hear the smirk in his voice. He *liked* me calling him that.

His hands drop down to my ass, and he squeezes, grinding his thick cock into my pussy, hard enough to make me moan.

"We're not going too fast?" he asks, trailing his lips across my jaw.

"No."

"Tell me what you want."

Before I can answer, the elevator doors open, and Xander pulls away from the wall.

"I want to walk."

"Do you?"

"Yeah. I want to see your place."

"Hmm. Maybe I want to take you—"

His words cut off, and he stills. He sniffs the air and growls.

It's not the sexy growl from earlier either.

"What is it?"

I barely get out the words before he's rushing me back inside the elevator. He pushes a button for the floor below, and when the doors open, another massive gargoyle is there waiting.

"Locheran," Xander says, handing me over as if I'm a child. "This is Evangeline. Protect her. Send Thorne and Elara to the penthouse."

I can't even protest being left in the arms of a stranger because Xander is back inside the elevator, the doors closing, before I'm able to process what's happening.

"Um..."

Locheran turns to walk down the hallway.

"Please put me down. I'm not a toddler."

"I don't know, you are kinda short," he muses, setting my feet on the ground.

"Says the man with horns and a tail."

"You can see my true form?"

"Am I not supposed to? I saw Xander as a gargoyle when we met."

"Interesting."

"What else am I supposed to see?"

He ignores the question and takes his phone out of his jeans pocket to make a call; I assume to the ones Xander told him to send to the penthouse.

I finally get a good look at this gargoyle.

He's got a similar build to Xander. Muscles for days. He's not as tall, that's for sure. I'd say he's a little over six feet. His hair is a lighter blue, and his skin is a darker shade of purple. Okay, are all gargoyles sexy?

Locheran isn't as sexy as Xander, though.

Ugh. Xander. I'm so confused right now.

The moment Locheran is done with his phone call, I plant my hands on my hips. "Can you tell me what the fuck is going on?"

He smiles briefly before his face drops back to serious. He waves his hand down the hallway to indicate we walk and talk. His palm finds my lower back, as if he's expecting me to run off and try to escape.

Not that I feel like a prisoner. What's crazy is I don't want to leave, even after what just happened.

"Xander sensed a threat."

"A threat? Does that happen a lot?"

"Not often, but he is a king, so it *does* happen."

"Xander is a king?" I ask, my voice an octave higher.

"Shit. He didn't tell you?"

"Um, no. He didn't. We literally just met."

Locheran stops in front of a door at the end of the tan and brown hallway. It's very drab and nondescript for a luxury apartment building.

"What are you, his guard or something?"

He smiles again and the skin crinkles around his violet eyes.

"I'm the commander of his army."

"Xander has an army?"

Locheran laughs this time. Glad he thinks I'm funny. "I'll let him explain everything."

He nods his chin at the door. "This is my apartment. It's warded. You'll be safe here."

"Is Xander's apartment not warded?"

He pauses before answering, carefully crafting his response. "It is, which means whatever got inside is more powerful than our shields."

"Shouldn't you be helping him?"

"I am merely following orders, and that involves protecting you."

"Seems like a waste of resources if you ask me."

He nudges me, and we walk inside. The doors automatically lock behind us.

What the hell? I've never seen technology like that before. It must be a rich person luxury.

Or something supernatural.

"You're sure these locks will hold? You say the place is warded but if the king's shields weren't strong enough, then how do you know yours are? And what do you mean by warded?"

"You sure ask a lot of questions, don't you?"

"Yeah. Start answering, Commander."

The nickname makes him smile again. He shakes his head as he walks into the kitchen. "Would you like something to drink?"

"Yes. I need booze."

He nods and extracts two glasses out of the cupboard, then grabs a bottle of whiskey and vodka from a cabinet. He holds them up, one in each hand, for me to choose.

"Vodka, please. Neat."

He fills the glass halfway and hands it to me. I choke it down and give the empty glass back for more.

He raises a brow, and I point at the glass. He shakes his head at me *again*.

"Don't judge me. I'm trying not to freak out here."

"Not judging. Just...entertained."

He hands me the refilled glass and sits down at the table across from me.

"So you're not freaking out. Why is that?" Locheran asks, eyeing me over his glass as he takes a drink of his whiskey. "Did you know of our existence before meeting Xander?"

"Yes and no. It's a long story."

"Would you like to share?" Locheran muses.

"Not really."

"Okay then."

I'm relaxed enough now to scope out the place. It's totally a bachelor's pad: empty white walls, bare minimum furniture, including a brown couch and recliner, a coffee table, and television mounted on the wall.

"You live here?"

"Yes."

"You should...paint. Hang some art or something."

"I should, huh?"

"Sorry, that was rude." I sigh. "Okay. Please tell me what's going on."

He takes a long draw of his liquor as he forms his answer. I assume he's going to leave out details. Maybe censor things a human shouldn't, or can't, know.

"The locks on the door are infused with the magic of our shields. Yes, they should work."

"Should?"

"They've worked up until now. There's never been a breach of our units or Xander's penthouse."

"Why now then?"

"He should really be telling you this."

I take two large gulps of my vodka and shake my head. "No. Either tell me, or I leave."

I won't, but he doesn't need to know that. I seem to be important to Xander for some reason even though we just met.

Locheran purses his lips. "Xander's wards are only as strong as he is. He's...weakening."

"Weakening? Why?"

He shifts in his seat as I refuse to break eye contact with him. "I can't tell you that. If you want to leave, then go. But that's not something for me to share."

"Is Xander sick?"

The commander is clearly uncomfortable. I want to keep pressing him, but I don't know this man. He's a supernatural being. What if I make him angry and he... attacks me?

Except, I don't sense malice from him, just like I didn't fear Xander harming me. I wish I could explain that. I finish the rest of my drink and jump out of my seat for another.

This vodka is starting to make me feel *real* good. Aside from the two frozen waffles for breakfast, I haven't had anything else to eat tonight. I kinda expected to be eating at a fancy restaurant right now with Xander, so I'm drinking on an empty stomach. Plus, I *rarely* drink, at least not the hard stuff. I'll have a glass of wine here and there.

Maybe I shouldn't have poured this third glass.

"Xander is on his way back now."

"What do you mean? How do you know? Did he text you? Or is it some gargoyle magic thing? Also, how do I address him? King Xander? Your Majesty? His Highness?"

I hiccup and giggle.

Shit. I might be tipsy.

Before Locheran can explain, Xander walks through the apartment door and rushes over to me.

"Are you okay?"

He cups my face in his hands and brushes a piece of hair out of my face. I swat his hand away, and he frowns.

"Yes, I'm fine," I say and take another swig of my vodka.

Xander stands up straight. "Are you drunk?"

I wave my finger at him. "No, sir. Just tipsy."

He glances at Locheran, who shrugs. "She's an adult. She can do whatever she wants."

"Leave him out of this. Tell me what's going on, Your Majesty."

Xander regards Locheran again, who shrugs for a second time.

"It slipped out."

Xander holds out his hand for me to take. "I'll explain everything."

I eye the hand, then gasp and grab it. "You have four fingers?"

I turn it over as if I'll find the fifth finger hiding some-where. How did I not notice this sooner? I suppose I don't count fingers on a human when first meeting them.

"We have four toes too," Locheran chuckles. I notice the scowl Xander gives him. "Well, four toes and a back claw."

"Shut up! No way!" I lean over, trying to get a view at either gargoyle's feet and nearly fall out of my chair.

"Evangeline," Xander barks, righting me in my chair and reeling me in from my amazement. His commanding voice speaks directly to my lust because all I want to do is behave.

"Please, come up to my penthouse. It's safe now, I promise."

"What was the threat? I want to know before going up there." I try to take another drink of vodka, but Xander grabs the glass from me and hands it to Locheran.

I cross my arms and pout.

"Kitten," Xander says, his voice soft.

"Kitten?" Locheran snorts. The king must give him a warning look because the commander straightens and clears his throat.

Xander palms my cheek. "I'm sorry I worried you. I had sensed something, but it wasn't inside the penthouse."

He drops his hand and turns to Locheran.

"The shields are intact, but the barrier outside the window to my living room was approached. The smell was off, as if it was disguising their scent to trick me. Thorne and Elara can give you the full report."

Xander turns back to me.

"Please, Evangeline, let me explain."

I should leave. This is crazy. I've just met the man and instead of us having an intimate night together, I'm being rushed out of his penthouse due to a threat.

Yet the idea of leaving makes me sick to my stomach.

I take his offered hand, and he leads me out of the apartment. I'm not sure if it's the vodka or the adrenaline pumping throughout my body, but my vision wavers, and I almost stumble to the ground. Xander notices and immediately scoops me into his arms like a groom carrying his bride over the threshold.

The elevator ride up one floor to the penthouse is quiet, and I rest my head on his chest, suddenly exhausted. I listen to his heart. It beats as fast as a high school drumline playing at a football half-time show. I'd say it's beating *too* fast, but maybe that's normal for gargoyles. Unless he's nervous. Why would he be? Because of me? That doesn't make sense. He's a king. I'm nobody.

He pauses just inside the penthouse to sniff the air and survey the space. He must be satisfied by what he finds because he continues walking until setting me down on a stool at the kitchen island.

He fills a glass with water and sets it in front of me.

"Drink all of it."

"Yes, sir."

I give him a wink and drink. While rehydrating, I scope out the place. It's mostly open concept. The kitchen is in a corner, with sleek metal appliances and marble counter-tops. There's a massive island in the middle with a table off to the right, big enough for four people. I assume the French doors past the table open to the dining room.

The living room is tall, at least two stories, with floor-to-ceiling windows and a breathtaking view of the Empire State Building.

Xander's apartment is also a bachelor pad but with more expensive taste. His couches are leather—or faux leather, I'm not sure. Chestnut hardwood floors, a rug with intricate designs. There's a fireplace with a television hanging above it. Artwork adorns one wall with another full of bookshelves. Books and odd collectible items fill the shelves.

I want to snoop. I wonder what types of books he likes to read.

When I finish my first glass of water, he refills it and hands it back.

"I'm ready to listen when you're ready to speak," I say, taking a drink. "Start with you being a king."

"I was going to tell you eventually. If tonight went well, that is. It's not really something you confess on a first date, you know?"

"Understandable."

"So, yes, I'm a king. I rule an army of gargoyles that protect New York City."

"Protect from what?"

"From evil."

"Is that what you sensed tonight? Outside your window? Something evil?"

"Yes."

"You think this evil wants to...what? Kill you? Take over the city?"

"Typically, yes."

"But?"

"There was something different about this being. I don't think it was here for me."

Chapter 6 - Xander

"What do you mean? Who was it here for?"

I could be wrong. I don't want to scare her, but there's no denying that something wanted to get through my barrier, which has never happened before. Not until I brought a human into my home.

"You said your mother told you about supernatural beings? That there are good and bad ones?"

She nods.

"The bad ones are able to disguise themselves as humans to find their victims. We protect the city the best that we can, but sometimes evil slips through, especially during the day."

"Why during the day?"

"Because the sun temporarily turns gargoyles to stone. We are not able to patrol, leaving our protective barriers vulnerable to an attack. Certain celestial and astronomical events also weaken our wards."

Her eyes widen, now fully invested. "What type of astronomical events?"

"Eclipses, meteor showers, All Hallow's Eve. The veil between worlds is thinnest during these occurrences, and it allows supernatural beings who are stronger to penetrate the shields."

"So, what kind of supernatural beings are we talking about?"

"Demons, rogue angels, creatures from the underworld."

She gasps. "What about vampires? Are they real? Werewolves?"

"Yes, though vampires and werewolves are not necessarily evil. Vampires can fall into bloodlust if they're not able to find a donor in time, and werewolves lose their humanity to silver poisoning."

"Fascinating. What about bigfoot? The Loch Ness monster?" She giggles, and I nudge the glass of water closer to her. She rolls her eyes but takes a sip.

"Bigfoot yes, but they stick to the forests. The Loch Ness monster, no one knows. I'm mostly talking about hellhounds, banshees, harpies…any mythological creature you can think of can have ill intent. Even gargoyles can become a threat. Me and my army sense any evil, and we defeat it before they can do harm or form a resistance large enough to bring down our shields."

"Locheran said *you* were becoming weaker."

I swipe my palm down my face. "He did, did he?"

"Why? Are you sick?"

My anger about Locheran spilling my secrets fades as I take in her concern. My hand finds her cheek again. I can't help it. I love touching her. Her skin is soft and warm. I want to tell her why I'm becoming weak, but I'm worried it will scare her away. What if she *is* my fated mate? If it is her destiny to be mine, she'd still have free will. She'd have to willingly accept me as her mate before we're able to perform the bonding ritual to bind our souls. But I don't want her to feel pressured if I tell her I could die if this does not happen.

"I'm weakening because I am approaching my thousandth year of living."

Somewhat true, just not the entire truth. I can only hope she won't hate me when I confess everything.

"One thousand," she whispers and hums.

I expected her to question me about my age, but she says nothing. Instead, she reaches for my hand, taking it in hers. Such a tiny hand compared to mine. Her touch is electrifying, and I hold my breath as she traces her fingertip over my palm, then across all four of my fingers and along my nails.

"They're so long and sharp."

I retract them, and she gasps. Many new things she discovers about me gets that reaction.

Nothing has scared her away yet.

Will she let me explore *her* body once we get over the night's excitement?

"I'm sorry you had to go through this tonight. Like I said, whatever tried to get through the barriers was after something. If it's you, then I need to know why."

"Me? But I'm just a human."

"You will never be 'just' anything. Never underestimate yourself, Evangeline. Not in your beauty, your career, or your life."

She lets out a long breath, her eyes filling with tears. One falls down her cheek, and she's quick to wipe it away.

"Sor–" She stops herself and smiles. "You're right. I am totally worth kidnapping."

I can't help the burst of laughter that bellows chest deep.

The amusement lighting up her face slowly fades.

"Wait," she says quietly and stands. "There's something else about the stories my mother used to tell me."

I'm curious about these stories. It's clearly why she wasn't afraid upon meeting me. She's been hearing about our existence her entire life. Then why did she act so shocked when I listed all the supernatural beings that exist?

Maybe her mother didn't provide those details. Or maybe it's the booze speaking. The water is helping, giving her a clear mind as we piece together the puzzle that is tonight.

"She used to tell me that something wanted to kidnap me. She'd adorn my crib with flowers—"

"Heathers? Like your tattoos? Is that why you got them?"

She nods. "My mother urged me to brand my body. She even recommended a friend to do it. It was a unique experience. The woman didn't speak English and during the entire tattoo session, she sang beautiful words."

A spell infused within the ink, as I suspected the moment we met.

"Anyway, I didn't question my mother's concern. I always believed her. My father, however, thought she was crazy. He sent her to a psychiatric hospital when I was ten. She's still there."

"Can you share some of these stories she told you?"

"Yes, but I'm convinced she held back a lot of details from me. Maybe because I was too young. I tried to get her to reveal more once I turned eighteen, but she was on so many meds, she could barely speak. She *still* doesn't talk much."

"We should visit her then. If she wanted you to get the tattoos of protection because she feared something was after you, then she must know more. We'll explain what happened tonight and maybe that will encourage her to give you all the details she left out. Anything that could provide some clarification on what could be hunting you and why."

Because it's possible I could be the reason she's in danger.

"Okay, but visiting hours are only Monday, Wednesday, and Friday, six a.m. until six p.m. I'd have to call to set up a special visitation after sunset. But like I said, I'm not sure how much help she'll be. On top of the meds, she's in her seventies now. Her memory isn't what it used to be."

I cross my arms, thinking.

"All we can do is try. When do you work again?"

"Tuesday."

"Is there any way I can convince you to take time off until we figure this out?"

"I..."

"Just think about it. I can help you with any finances—"

"I couldn't."

"If it means you're safe, then I insist."

She scrunches up her nose, and I stop myself from telling her that I will give her anything she could ever dream of, because I realize how crazy that sounds being we just met.

"Is your mother's hospital located here in the city?"

"No. About an hour and a half outside."

"Fuck."

"What?"

"I'm afraid I can't go with you then. As king, I'm tethered to this city. I can only fly a mile or two outside of the limits. I'll send Locheran in my place."

The thought of not having her near me already sparks a ball of panic deep within my soul. However, I trust my commander.

She opens her mouth to argue, but I hold up my finger.

"You need to go, and I must stay and protect this city. Locheran is my most trusted soldier. He will keep you safe. I'll send a team of soldiers with you two as well. Monday at sunset, he'll fly you up there."

She considers my words and eventually relents. Still, her eyebrows pinch together.

"Do we have to fly? Won't it be weird if Locheran and I show up without a car? And I'm not about to walk in with wind-whipped hair. I'd rather drive or take the train."

Right. She's 'not a fan' of heights. I suppose they should go the boring human route. While no one would notice if they showed up without a car, she might be right on the wind-whipped hair. I like to keep mine braided when flying.

"I'll hire a car for you two. I don't trust trains. Too public. I'll have a few soldiers fly up there to scope out the place, make sure there's no danger before you arrive. The rest will escort the car."

"You're wasting too many resources on me."

I tsk at her.

"Oh, Kitten. You are not, and never will be, a waste. And if you keep doubting yourself around me, I will have my soldiers find the fucker who convinced you that you're not worthy. I'll rip their spine out of their body and feed their flesh to the hellhounds that prowl at the gate between Hell and Earth's realm."

Her mouth hangs open, her eyes wide. "Jesus, Xander."

"I apologize if that was too detailed and violent for you—"

"Um, no. That was...hot."

She giggles, and the sound warms my chest with pride.

"I know that's not a normal reaction, but I've never had anyone offer to murder someone for me. I'm...flattered. Does that make me weird?"

I brush a piece of her hair behind her ear, and she blushes at the move. "No. But even if it did, I like weird."

She yawns, her eyes struggling to stay open. Despite how badly I want to hear more about how me violently killing someone in her honor pleases her, she needs sleep.

"Let me prepare the guest room for you."

"I can go home."

"No. Not if something is targeting you."

"I have my cat at my apartment. I need clothes, personal items..."

"I'll send someone to get your belongings and the cat."

"Her name is Birdie."

"I'll send someone to get Birdie then."

Locheran is going to kill me. He's scared of cats. I remind him he's a six-foot three, three-hundred-pound gargoyle, but I can never convince him he's safe from being killed by a cat.

The odds are low, but never zero, he'd say.

I fire off a text to him and ask Evangeline for her keys. While waiting for Locheran to arrive, I lead my tired kitten to the room where she'll be staying. She pauses at the door.

"What if I want to stay in your room with you? So you can protect me."

She glances up at me with those doe eyes and fluttering lashes again. They're a weapon, I swear.

I plant my hand on the doorframe and lean into her. She holds her breath. "I'm afraid I wouldn't be able to keep my hands to myself if you shared a bed with me. And while that is what we had intended to do when coming back to my place tonight, you're tired, and what I have planned for you will take all night. You need to rest. Tomorrow we can play."

Before she can argue, I turn to a closet outside of the bathroom across the hall from her room.

"Towels and toiletries are in here. I'll get you some clothes to sleep in for tonight."

I sense Locheran at the penthouse door and excuse myself, despite how much I don't want to leave her side.

"Kitten's keys," Locheran says when I open the door, his hand held out and a smirk on his stupid face.

"You're enjoying this, aren't you?"

I slap the keys into his palm and try to close the door. He sticks his foot inside to stop it.

"Do you think she's the one?" he asks.

"It would explain a lot of things. Like why she's seeing our true forms."

"Don't fuck it up," he quips, and I narrow my eyes at him. He bows. "Your Majesty."

"Get the fuck out. I'll text you her address."

"Fuck you for sending me to get a cat," Locheran yells as I close the door in his face.

When I return to the guest room, the door is open, and I hear the shower running in the bathroom across the hall.

I set a pair of my sweats and a t-shirt on her bed and prepare her a sandwich with chips and a glass of water. I didn't get a chance to take her out to dinner. I had planned a beautiful date beginning with a meal at my favorite French restaurant, a walk along the Hudson River underneath the night sky, and multiple orgasms to end the night.

Instead, I have a possible fated mate who is being targeted, likely because of me.

I shower as well and dress in a similar outfit to the one I chose for Evangeline. The thought of her wearing my clothes awakens my cock. Now that the danger is over, at least for now, I'd love nothing more than to ravish her. But I must be patient. She's too tired tonight.

I walk out of my bedroom at the same time she does from the guest room.

"Hi," she says shyly.

"Hello, Kitten."

Her cheeks blush at the nickname. *She loves it.* I take a step towards her.

"I left you something to eat."

"Thank you. I just finished it. I love turkey sandwiches." She matches my step with one of her own. Her eyes dart around my body, to my horns, my mouth, my arms, down to my four-toed feet. "Can I..."

She looks away and plays with a wet strand of her brown hair.

"What is it, Evangeline?"

"Can I touch you?" She grimaces. "Innocently, I mean. It's just...I have this overwhelming urge—or *need*—to touch you."

She shakes her head.

"That's dumb. I'm sor—" Her nose crinkles, almost saying the word I've scolded her not to use.

"It's not dumb. You can do whatever you'd like to me—*with* me."

She smiles and moves closer. Raising her hand, she places it on my stomach and runs it up my abs to my chest. I hold back my growl because if I let it out now, I'll grab her and hold her against the wall while I slam my cock into her wet pussy.

The smell of her arousal is intoxicating.

Her palm smooths over my chest, and I wish I hadn't put on this damn shirt so I can feel her skin slide over my own.

She walks around me, and I hear her suck in a sharp breath.

"Your wings," she whispers, finding them tucked to my back. "They're purple too, but a darker shade."

"Would you like to see them?" I ask and turn to face her. She nods.

"Come here."

I take her hand and lead her to the living room where there's more space.

"Are you ready?" I ask with a smile.

She nods, and I extract my wings. They shoot out, expanding twenty feet from end to end.

Evangeline gasps and places her palm on her chest.

"They're so big," she whispers. The words make my cock twitch. "Can I touch them?"

I pause before answering. I've never let anyone touch them before. My wings are my lifeline. If I lose them, if they're damaged, I couldn't fly. I wouldn't be able to defend my kingdom.

"You don't have to..."

"No, that's not it. It's just...I've never let anyone."

"It's okay–"

"Kitten," I say, barely able to contain how much I *need* her to touch my wings. "Come over here."

She slowly walks to where I stand in the middle of the living room.

"You can touch them. I *want* you to."

"Are you sure? We just met, and it seems like things are going way too fast. I mean, I messaged you for a one-night stand and the moment I saw you, I knew it wasn't going to be that. And I can't explain why."

I can, but not right now. I don't want to ruin this moment.

"I feel the same way. Sometimes our bodies don't listen to reason. And that's okay."

She smiles. "What will happen when I touch your wings?"

I shrug, even though I know. "Let's find out."

She walks to my side and lifts her hand. She gives me one last glance, and I nod my approval.

The moment her palm grazes the thin, silky membrane, I let out a moan. She pulls her hand back as if it burned.

"Oh," she breathes out. "Is that supposed to happen?"

I wrap my wings around her, cocooning her body, and cup her face in my hands.

"With you? Yes."

I kiss her.

Our first kiss.

Her soft lips meld into mine, plump and eager as they open to let my tongue slide in. She tastes like cinnamon.

Her hands smooth down my chest, her fingertips teasing the hem of my shirt before she slips them underneath the fabric. My cock jerks the moment her warm palms cover my abs.

The kiss intensifies the more she touches me. It's as if every part of her that makes contact with me sends currents through my veins. Electricity fills the air with every stroke of my tongue over hers.

She moans into my mouth, and my fingers move to the back of her head to clutch her hair, still damp from her shower. I fist the strands, tugging roughly as I deepen the kiss.

She feels so good.

She's making me feral.

A beast.

She gasps, and I stop.

"Too much?" I ask, out of breath.

"No, harder," she responds, just as breathless.

Her fingertips skim over my wings again, and I nearly come undone.

I let out an animalistic growl and take her ass in my hands to lift her. Her legs automatically go around my waist.

"I know you're exhausted—"

"I'm not."

"I was going to let you sleep—"

"I'm not tired."

"But if I don't taste you right now, I might lose my goddamn mind."

"Then taste me, Your Majesty."

She doesn't have to tell me twice.

Chapter 7 - Evangeline

My beast.

Xander carries me to his bedroom, which has a gothic vibe. Black walls, dresser, and dark hardwood floors. Silver bedding to match the silver chandelier hanging from the vaulted black ceiling. Even his paintings mounted on the wall are black and silver.

He gently sets me on the ground and takes a step back to scan my body from head to toe.

"I just want to appreciate how beautiful you look."

I glance down. The t-shirt is slightly too small and clings to my tummy. His sweats barely fit, too, as my ass is wider.

Brandon never complimented me. Ever. I didn't realize how odd that was until my fortieth birthday, when men were complimenting me left and right. I didn't realize how much I needed the validation.

I needed it then, but now, I'm at the point in loving myself and my body that hearing Xander say those words sends a shot of dopamine through my veins. He's a fucking gargoyle king who looks like a God sent from...heaven?

Where do gargoyles come from?

It doesn't matter. He called me beautiful, and he *means* it.

"Why do you never believe the things I say to you? Who hurt you to make you feel as if you're not a goddess who walks the land?"

Goddess. His words are cheesy, but my pussy is eating it up. She's pulsing and wet and I'm dying to let this gargoyle king do ungodly things to me.

"Whatever you're thinking about, keep it up," he says, sniffing the air.

I squeeze my thighs together.

I love that he can smell how turned on I am.

"Tell me what you want me to do to you. What do you like?"

"I...I don't know. I don't have much experience."

He steps closer to me.

"Why?"

I gulp, trying to wet my dried-out throat.

"Well, I was married, and he's the only man I've slept with. Then we got divorced, and I've been too scared to have sex with anyone else yet because my sex life with my ex was...bland."

"Did he make you come?"

"No. I'd go to the bathroom after and finish myself off."

"Oh, Kitten, I'm going to enjoy showing you what you've been missing."

He holds up his hand and retracts his claws, then teases the band of my sweats—*his* sweats—with his fingertips.

"Do you want me to eat this sweet pussy and make you come on my tongue?"

I whimper, and he gives me a knowing smirk. He said exactly what I needed to hear.

"Did your ex ever go down on you?"

"Yes, but he hated it. He wasn't good either, and I had to fake my orgasms."

He tsks and slides his hand down my front until his fingertip teases my slick opening.

"Hold on to me, okay?"

I nod and clutch his arms and nearly collapse to the ground when he eases a finger inside me. His digit is long and thick, and my pussy clenches around it.

I moan, and he leans down to capture it with a kiss.

The moment his lips meet mine, he pumps his finger in and out, slowly...torturously. His tongue gently massages my own, as if he's savoring the taste.

He adds a second finger, pausing to let me stretch around him before thrusting into me faster. My knees become weak, and I grip his arms harder for leverage.

I've never felt such *pleasure* solely from a hand.

He breaks off the kiss to clutch my hair at the nape, tugging to pull back my head so he can trail his mouth over my jaw and neck...all while he pumps his fingers inside me.

"Xander, please, I'm getting close."

"Good. Come for me, Kitten."

His fangs scratch over the valley between my neck and shoulder, and his thumb presses against my clit.

That's the moment I fall apart.

I hold on to him as I scream and shake and let the orgasm wash over me.

His fingers stay paused inside me, my pussy pulsing around them.

When I finally come down from that mind-blowing orgasm, he pulls his fingers out and brings them up to his mouth.

He licks them clean.

I've never witnessed anything so *intimate.*

Brandon always complained about going down on me. He said it was gross and unsanitary.

Yet this gargoyle —this *king*—sucks my release off his fingers as if I'm dessert after a three-course meal.

"You taste so sweet, Kitten. Let's lie you down so I can have more."

He walks us to the bed, my thighs brushing up against the edge.

"Lift your arms."

He pulls the t-shirt over my head and tosses it behind him to the ground. Next, he removes my sweats until I'm left standing there in nothing but my panties.

"So fucking gorgeous, Evangeline."

His large hand cups a breast. It's so small in his palm. His thumb flicks my hard, sensitive nipple, and I groan.

"I love how you react to my touch," he says, his voice low and seductive.

He bends down to remove my panties next, and I hold onto his shoulders to step out of them.

"Get on the bed."

God, why do I love him giving me orders? All I want to do is behave and be a good girl for him.

I get on the bed and scoot back, propping myself up with my elbows to watch him undress.

"How do clothes work with your wings and tail?"

"Magic-infused fabric." He turns as he takes off his shirt, allowing me to see the fabric separate when it slides past the wings. It weaves back together once it's off his body.

"Whoa," I whisper.

Xander grins from ear to ear, and his tail whips back and forth. There's something on the end that I can't quite make out, but it's shaped somewhat like a flower's bud. Bulb shaped, even.

My nipples tighten painfully hard thinking about what he could do to me with that tail.

He kneels on the floor. He's so tall, the edge of the bed barely reaches his stomach. He grabs me by the hips and tugs me down, allowing him to wrap his arms around my thighs and spread my legs apart.

"You're still so wet for me, Evangeline. I can't wait to have this inside you."

He sticks out his tongue. I whimper at the sight because it's a long fucking tongue. It extends down his chin and appears to be at least seven inches.

He must like my reaction because his tail whips around behind his back again.

"I want you to play with your nipples while I eat you out, okay? I want to hear you scream. Show your king how well he devours you."

Your king.

He laps his tongue up my pussy to my clit, and I try to close my legs around his head on instinct.

"No, Kitten. You keep these open for me."

He takes my clit into his mouth and sucks, causing me to buck.

"You're not touching yourself."

My hands move to my breasts, and I take my nipples between my thumb and index finger. I pinch them, twist them, pull on them hard, all while Xander drags his teeth over my clit.

My back arches off the bed, and he pushes me back down with the tips of his wings.

"You're doing so well, Evangeline."

I groan at his praise. Why was that so fucking hot?

He glides his tongue back down my slit and then without warning, he thrusts it inside me.

I scream and try to arch my back again, but his wings are there to stop me.

Fuck, that feels so good.

He pumps his long, thick tongue in and out of me at a casual pace.

"Faster, harder," I wheeze.

He picks up speed and presses a finger down on my clit, adding just enough pressure while massaging it to nearly send me over the edge.

When he removes his finger from the sensitive bundle of nerves, I whine. Only seconds later, the pressure is back.

But it's not his fingers. It's the end of his tail. It presses up against my clit and starts *vibrating*. No fucking way.

"Oh, God, Xander. Yes. That feels...that feels..."

My words are lost as an orgasm claims my voice. He doesn't let me get through it this time before he's back to fucking me with that glorious tongue. The bulb-shaped tail presses down harder, still vibrating.

He's going to make me come for a third time.

The tip of his finger teases my asshole. I've never had anyone there, not a cock or a finger. My ex would never try it.

"Yes."

It's all I say, and Xander swipes his finger through my pleasure for lubricant, then eases the tip past the outer ring.

"Fuck, oh God."

It's too much. Another orgasm is already building. Between him driving into me with his long, thick tongue, his vibrating tail, the wings holding me down, me tugging on my hard, sensitive nipples, and his finger inside my asshole, I come.

I scream loud enough that I worry the entire building heard.

Xander comes up for air with a goofy smile on his face, almost as if he got high on eating me out.

"So good, Kitten." He kisses up my body, from my fupa to my soft stomach and between my breasts, leaving sweet pecks along my collarbone. "We'll need to get that tight little hole stretched so I can fuck it with my tail."

I groan.

He brushes his mouth over my lips. "You taste like nectar."

He kisses me, and I open for him, tasting myself on his tongue. *It does taste like nectar.* The kiss isn't long, but I'm burning up by the time he pulls away and stands. Desire that should have been satiated after three orgasms begs for more.

My eyes fall to the tent in his sweats.

I move to take care of it, and he stops me.

"Not yet, Kitten. My cock isn't like a human's."

"It's okay."

"I know...but just watch me tonight, okay?"

Chapter 8 - Xander

I drop my sweats, and Evangeline's eyes widen.

Gargoyle cocks are long and thick and bulbous throughout. The tip extends, curving to stimulate the G-spot or the prostate. And the base expands at the height of pleasure, knotting inside to make sure all my seed is spent and not one drop is wasted.

Like my tail, my cock can also vibrate to enhance my partner's experience.

Evangeline's pussy was neglected by that low-life of an ex, and I'm determined to make it right. But first, we need to stretch her out, prepare all her holes so she solely feels pleasure.

She should only feel pain if she asks for it.

She seems to like it rough. I'd love to tie her up and let my cock, tail, and wings fuck all her holes.

My fingers wrap around my shaft, and I squeeze before fisting up and down the length. Pre-cum leaks out of the tip.

Evangeline sits on the edge of the bed and watches like a good girl. She licks her lips, and her hands clutch the sheets.

She desperately wants to touch me, to have me in her mouth.

My strokes are slow because if I go any faster, I'll come. I'm too worked up after making Evangeline orgasm thrice. I keep remembering her sounds, her whimpers and moans caused by *me*...yeah, I'm not going to last long.

"Come on me, Xander. Come in my mouth. Wherever you like," she says, clearly seeing that I'm close to losing it.

"Fuck, why are you perfect?" I grind out.

I speed up my fisting, and Evangeline sticks out her tongue, begging to have my release in her mouth.

A beautiful sight that sends me over the edge.

I should warn her, but it's too late. I come. Thick ropes fall on her tongue and chin, down to her breasts and stomach.

It's...a lot of fucking cum.

Evangeline swipes her finger through the jizz on her chin and shoves it in her mouth.

Her eyes widen. "Holy shit. Why does it taste so good?"

Her words make my heart kick in my chest. I can't tell her that it's likely because she's my fated mate. It's too soon, and I don't want to scare her away.

I first suspected it the moment we met. It explains why I feel such an intense attraction to her. I mean, just her photo on the dating app took my breath away.

But then we met in person...the way my heart felt as if it was being ripped from my chest because if she's my mate, my heart belongs to her. The way she can see my true form, which no human should be able to do. If she's my mate, no gargoyle masking will work against her.

And now...the way she takes pleasure in my *pleasure*... her cunt was delectable, better than any partner I've ever had. Sex between mates is always heightened, the bond nearly making us addicted to each other.

It will only become stronger if she accepts me, and we bind our souls together.

"Come on," I say and hold out my hand. "Let's clean you up."

I lead her to the shower where I wash off my cum. I keep it quick, because after three orgasms, she's barely able to keep her eyes open.

She was exhausted before, and I had every intention to let her rest after the earlier scare, but I lost all control when she showed interest in me, in my body, my wings...touching them and making my cock painfully hard. My wings being highly sensitive to her touch is another sign she's my mate.

I dress her in the same sweats and t-shirt from before and lead her to her room.

"Wait. I want to sleep in your bed."

I don't argue because I can no longer deny her what she wants.

The moment I tuck her into my king-size bed, she falls asleep. I watch her for a few minutes and wonder what supernatural being wants to cause her harm. Why would they be after her?

The only answer that makes sense is me. If my potential fated mate is killed before we unite our souls, then I am as good as dead.

Evangeline is so fragile as most humans are. I'll protect her, though. I just need to know what I'm up against. Maybe we can get some answers from her mother on Monday.

I wake with a stretch and a yawn, realizing that was the best sleep I've had in centuries. I reach for my kitten, only to realize she's not there, and the mattress is cold.

My heart begins racing, worried she has left me, or perhaps she was taken by the creature I sensed outside the barriers last night. Were they able to get through?

It's not until I hear her hearty laughter coming from the kitchen that my anxious thoughts subside. Locheran's voice follows, and an emotion I've never felt before rises within my body.

Jealousy.

I slip out of bed and march out to the kitchen where the two sit at the island.

"Whoa, buddy," Locheran begins. "You've got murder on your face. Are we going demon hunting?"

Evangeline's eyes widen, and her mouth forms a perfect 'O'. Locheran's words should have concerned her, but instead, she seems intrigued.

"No, wait," Locheran says, his mouth twisting into a malicious grin. "I know what's happening."

"What?" Evangeline asks, her face twisting in confusion.

Locheran throws up his hands. "Look, Xanny. I'm just here to deliver a cat."

That's when I notice a black cat on my marble countertop eating wet food. It glances up at me and slow-blinks before resuming its meal.

"Sorry about her being on the countertop. I'll wipe it down. She's very picky about where she eats. I have to feed her like this at my apartment."

Evangeline chews on her bottom lip, worried about my reaction. I suppose I still have a territorial mask on my face. I knew this would happen the moment I tasted her. The need to make her mine, to protect and defend her from other gargoyles, kicked in.

It will only get worse the more we give in to the bond.

Locheran knows this. He's testing me, the asshole.

"Do not be sorry, Kitten. The cat can be on the counter."

"Birdie. That's her name."

"Right. Birdie."

I turn my attention to Locheran. "You should go."

"Xander," Evangeline gasps. "That wasn't very nice. The commander and I were enjoying our breakfast and talking about our favorite zombie movies and TV shows."

She places her palm on top of his knuckles, and I fist my hands at my side.

"You can stay," she says to Locheran, who notices my building fury.

"Uh…" He stands and sets his dishes in the sink. "I actually have to go. I forgot I have a meeting to attend."

He pauses next to me before leaving.

"Tone it down, buddy. You don't want to scare her away."

I breathe in deeply, then slowly let out the breath. The moment Locheran is gone, that territorial fight subsides.

"What the hell was that about?" Evangeline asks, standing to put her dirty dishes in the sink. "Why did Locheran lie about having a meeting and rush out of here so fast?"

"How do you know he was lying?"

"Because he told me he had no plans today. Plus, I just somehow knew he was lying."

She could probably sense or taste his deception, another side effect of being my fated mate. I can taste the lies of my soldiers.

I walk to the coffee machine to pour myself a cup of much needed caffeine.

"Maybe he could sense how hungry I am right now." I watch her over the top of my mug. She's leaning against the kitchen island, arms crossed, brows pinched. Her adorable button nose scrunches.

"Then eat something. Locheran made breakfast. Scrambled eggs, bacon, and toast."

"I'm not talking about that type of breakfast, Kitten."

Her mouth falls open, and her eyes widen. "Oh."

She squirms on her feet, and the heavenly scent of her arousal hits my nose. Good. Maybe she'll forget about me acting like a possessive asshole when I make her scream my name.

I set my mug down and stalk toward her, caging her in between my long arms.

"I'm starving, Evangeline. I want to lay you down on this countertop and devour your delectable cunt," I whisper next to her ear. She shivers as my hot breath brushes against her skin. "I want to hear your screams of pleasure when my mouth makes you come. Then, once you're done shaking from your release, I'll do it again because you deserve all the orgasms your asshole ex failed to give you."

"What if I want you to fuck me on this counter?"

I growl, and her eyes light up at her favorite sound. "You're not ready for my cock, Kitten. I need you to be patient. Can you do that for your king?"

She answers by slipping off her sweats and panties and climbing on top of the counter.

Her cat lifts its head from the bowl of food, and the smart thing must realize what's about to happen because it jumps down and disappears somewhere inside the pent-house.

"I can be patient."

She moves her hand down to touch her clit, and I swat it away.

"No, Evangeline. Your pleasure is *mine*. You will never be forced to come by your hand or by any toy ever again. Not unless I'm the one ordering you to touch yourself. Not unless I'm the one holding the toy."

She whimpers, clearly liking the sound of that.

I sit down on a stool, placing myself perfectly in front of Evangeline's pussy. I lean in and inhale deeply.

"If I could bottle the delicious scent of your cunt, I would."

Then I wrap my arms around her thick thighs and dive in.

Chapter 9 - Evangeline

Xander's long, thick tongue licks up my pussy lips, and I moan my appreciation. He takes my clit in his mouth and sucks hard, forcing me to arch off the marble countertop. His wings swoop in, pushing me back down.

He's done that before, and the move heightens my pleasure in a way I can't explain.

I need more. I reach down to grab Xander's horns and pull him closer. He must sense what I'm asking for because his tongue dips inside me, and I groan as it expands to fit my pussy.

What the hell? His tongue grows?

"Yes, Kitten, it grows."

Oops. Didn't realize I asked that out loud. Why didn't he do that the first time he went down on me? I suppose last night was already...overwhelming.

He's thrusting his meaty tongue in and out of me at a casual pace. He loves savoring me—my *taste*. I tug on his horns again, needing him to go faster.

"Patience, Evangeline," he mumbles, then gets back to work.

Xander's wings somehow peel my hands off his horns and pins them above my head.

Oh. OH. I like this.

I squirm beneath him, and the wings press down harder, making sure I'm not going anywhere.

While Xander's tongue works my greedy cunt, his bulbous tail presses on the sensitive bundle of nerves and starts vibrating.

"Oh, fuck, Xander, please."

His hands slip underneath my shirt to my tits—I'm not wearing a bra—and he takes both nipples between his fingers, twisting and pinching and nearly sending me over the edge.

It feels like I'm being fucked by more than one person. The overstimulation is euphoric, sending me into a state of ecstasy.

No other man—being—will ever be good enough.

His mouth ravages me. His hands worship me. And that vibrating tail applies the perfect amount of pressure, as if he's able to read my thoughts and know what I want.

Come for me, Kitten.

It was Xander's voice, but he didn't speak those words out loud, because he never took his mouth off my cunt.

Still, the command is my undoing. My back arches off the countertop, and my entire body shakes as I climax.

Once I'm done, Xander removes his tongue, and his wings release my arms. He crawls up my body and hovers over me, making sure to keep his weight off me.

He smiles, his fangs showing. Did he have them out the entire time while eating me out? If so, I never felt them scrape against me.

I watch, eyes wide, as the pointed teeth slowly retract.

Oh. So he can control them?

"They like to slide out when I'm...turned on."

He must have seen the confusion on my face.

"When you're ready, I can use them on you to enhance your pleasure."

"Use them on me? Do you mean...bite me? Like a vampire?"

"Yes."

"You'll drink my blood?"

"I keep telling you I'm a beast, Evangeline. I consume blood."

Why am I not disgusted by this? "Have you ever killed ...um..."

"A human? Yes, but no one who was innocent. Did I eat them? No. Flesh is not my taste. But the fangs are there for a reason, and I've used them to kill and devour blood.

"Now," he continues. "I'm going to kiss you, because I never want you to forget how fucking good you taste, okay?"

I nod.

His mouth crashes with mine. His tongue slips past my lips and massages my own. I whimper because I taste just as good as I did last night.

A subtle sweetness. It's a different taste from Xander's cum. He's sweeter *and* saltier.

How is this possible?

I have a lot of questions, but Xander's being cautious about answering some of them. I want to push him to tell me, but at the same time, I'm hesitant. I'm having so much fun with this gargoyle king. What if his secrets scare me away?

Nothing's scared me away yet.

I signed up for *Kis-meet* because I wanted a fling. Not a commitment.

Yet, here I am, desperately needing more of this super-natural hottie despite us meeting only last night. It feels like it's been weeks.

Xander breaks off the kiss and cups my cheek. "What's wrong? Are you okay?"

Did he sense my mood change? Can he see the doubt on my face?

"I'm fine."

I move to sit up, and he jumps off the countertop and helps me get down.

"Evangeline—"

"Xander, I..." I take a deep breath because I'm not sure what I'm trying to say...or where this is suddenly coming from. Everything was fine, but my overactive brain decided to make an appearance. "I'm just freaking out a little."

He smiles, his silver eyes softening. It's a strange thing to see on such an intimidating creature.

"I understand how rushed this all may seem. We will go as fast or slow as you want. You will find us gargoyles are patient. We are trained to stand still for hours upon hours."

My heart warms with his words. He always says the right things. He has all the green flags.

"I want to do *everything* with you," I begin, "but at the same time, it scares me how much I *need* you. This was only supposed to be a one-night stand, and here we are, on night two. I mean, you moved my cat in. Locheran brought over my clothes and some personal belongings."

I bend over to grab my pants that fell to the floor, and Xander helps me put them on because he's a good man who likes taking care of me.

Yet another thing that scares me because I've never felt so...appreciated in my life. A part of my brain is convincing me I don't deserve it, which confuses me because that's my old life speaking. That's not who I am anymore.

"I know you're protecting me from whatever thing approached your shield. I'm hoping my mom can help answer questions about that...but as for everything else that's happening between us...you're going to need to explain."

I hold up my hand when he opens his mouth.

"Not right now. I don't think my stress will allow it. Tomorrow, after I get back from visiting my mother. Until then...can we slow down?"

He takes my face between his hands and nuzzles his nose with mine. Ugh. Why is he so cute?

"Anything for you. Anything you want. You're in charge here."

I laugh. "I am?"

"Absolutely."

His tail whips back and forth behind him. I've noticed it does that when he's happy, or excited...or turned on.

Xander's phone rings, interrupting our moment. He sees the name on the screen, and his face immediately drops into a regal mask. Damn, why is that sexy? Okay, I'm horny as hell, despite Xander making me come just minutes ago.

I have no doubt that there's something magical bringing us together. It's the only explanation as to why our connection is so...*intense*. I still can't get over the fact that a king could be mine. A *king*.

"I have business to take care of. I'll likely be gone for the rest of the night. Make yourself at home. I'll have two soldiers, Thorne and Elara, stationed outside the penthouse doors. If you need anything, anything at all, let them know. I have patrols sweeping the area outside as well."

He's thought of everything to protect me from the thing that wants to kidnap me. Or kill me. I still can't understand why me. I'm really not special.

Unless...it's less about hurting me and more about going through me to harm the gargoyle king.

X ander was gone the rest of the night.

I killed time by catching up on TV shows while cuddling with Birdie. That got boring after a while, so I tried chatting with Thorne and Elara stationed outside the penthouse door.

Neither one is the chatty type.

Thorne at least attempted to be friendly when I asked the two about their lives and what it's like working for Xander. Elara, however, kept huffing and rolling her eyes.

"You're distracting us from our jobs, human," she said.

Rude.

Giving up trying to charm the stern soldiers, I went back inside the penthouse.

I vaguely remember Xander returning minutes before sunrise to find me asleep in his bed, taking me in his arms, and kissing my neck before his loud chainsaw snores filled the room.

My sleep is restless, which tends to happen the night before visiting my mother, and I wake up a few hours before sunset. I'm tempted to wake Xander to keep me company, but he looks too peaceful right now.

I keep myself busy by making breakfast: scrambled eggs, bacon, and toast. Xander's fridge stays stocked, and I'm wondering if he knows how to cook...as if he could get any sexier.

After eating, I shower and dress for the day, then Birdie and I hang out on the couch while I doom scroll social media for half an hour.

Locheran finally knocks on the door right at seven p.m.

"Hey," he says, rubbing his eyes. He yawns, flashing his white fangs and stretching his long wings. "Ready to go?"

"Yeah. I was hoping Xander would be awake by now so I can say goodbye—"

"Or kiss him goodbye?" he teases.

"Or fuck him goodbye?" I counter, making Locheran blush. "Does he usually sleep this much? Did he have a long night?"

Locheran pauses at my questions.

"Is he sleeping longer because of what you told me about him weakening?"

"Always asking me questions that Xander should be answering." He waves me toward the door. "Come on. The sooner we leave, the faster you can return to your king."

Now I'm the one to blush, and I bite my lip, staring longingly at the hallway toward Xander's room. I must stand there longer than I realize because Locheran sighs and pulls on my arm, forcing me out of the penthouse.

"I have a question."

It's barely five minutes into the car ride, and I'm already bored. Locheran doesn't respond, maybe because he hates it when I ask him questions.

"The fangs. Yours seem to stay out all the time. Xander keeps his hidden unless he's turned on. Why is that?"

"Maybe I'm always turned on and that's why mine stay down."

I fake a gag. "Gross."

He sighs dramatically.

"Every gargoyle is different. Some keep them sheathed, others do not. *I* think mine are sexy, therefore *I* keep mine out." He smiles, flashing his fangs to solidify his point. "Any more questions?"

I open my mouth, because I do have more questions, but Locheran's phone interrupts me. For the next few minutes, I watch him juggle between texting someone nonstop and making phone calls to bark out orders to the team of gargoyles escorting us out of the city. They're relaying information back to him that I've tuned out because if I hear them talking about their mission of protecting me, I might just stress out more than I already am.

Xander texts me a few times, checking in. He's mad I didn't wake him to say goodbye and made me promise to make it up to him when I get back.

I know he's worried since he couldn't come with us.

"So, Xander is tethered to the city, but you and the rest of his army are not?" I ask once Locheran is done with all his calls.

"Correct."

"How long has he been stranded here?"

"He's not stranded—" Locheran pinches his nose and sighs. "He's been here since the early 1600s."

"Seriously? Damn." I stare out the window, watching the city skyline disappear into the night the further we drive. "What was his deal yesterday at breakfast?"

"Are you going to ask me questions this entire trip? Because I will launch myself out of the car into traffic."

"Rude."

"I'm sorry, it's just...when Xander is weak, we can all feel his exhaustion."

"Does that affect your ability to protect the city?"

"Not yet, but..."

"But you worry it will only get worse the closer he gets to his birthday."

He nods and leans his head back on the headrest.

"I'm sorry, Locheran."

I place my hand on his forearm, and his eyes pop open.

"Whoa. That was weird."

"What?"

"You, like, sent a dose of calm throughout my body."

I pull my hand back and open my palms, staring down at them. "I did? How?"

"You sure you're human?"

"Yes?"

"It must be the fate—"

He clears his throat and takes out his phone, pretending to answer a call.

"The what!?"

He points at the phone and starts talking, but I know he's faking it to avoid answering my question. Fine. I'll just add it to the list of things to ask Xander.

Now I'm mad at the commander, so I cross my arms and stare out the window for the rest of the trip. He tries to start a conversation with me a few times, but I only shrug or give him one-word answers.

Locheran has quickly become the sibling I never had. He's a handsome gargoyle, but I have no attraction to him whatsoever. He feels more like a brother to me.

It takes us a little over an hour to get to the town of Montgomery, where my mother's psychiatric hospital is located.

I'm never here this late, and it's creepy as hell. The hallways are empty, as most patients are already in bed for the night. I called ahead to schedule a special visitation, making sure they wouldn't let my mom fall asleep before we got here.

Locheran and I sit in the visitor's room, which reminds me of a prison. There are cafeteria style tables set up throughout. Bars cover all the windows. The walls are bland, and it smells like a mix of pee, bleach, and death.

"Well, this is depressing," Locheran murmurs out of the side of his mouth.

"Yep."

I freaked out a little when we walked in, forgetting that only I can see the gargoyles in their true form. Locheran assured me he's masked as a six-foot-three human with short black hair, blue eyes, and a smile that could charm the panties off any woman.

Unnecessary comment, but in the short time I've known Locheran, I've learned he's a bit of a playboy. I'm determined to find him someone to settle down with. I wonder if he'd be into a gorgeous plus-size baddie named Farrah aka my bestie.

After a few minutes of waiting, two guards enter with my mother, holding her up by both of her arms. I almost expected her to be in cuffs with the way this place is run. Instead, she looks drugged out and that's why they're basically dragging her in here.

My mother, Mira, has always been a large woman like me. Now she's wasted away. She's *been* wasting away since the day my father threw her in here. We used to look identical. Our brown hair and blue eyes, chubby cheeks and round bodies. Now, she's lost at least seventy-five pounds.

The guards sit her down in the seat across from us and walk away to stand guard against the wall. Well, I say they're standing guard, but both men pull out their phones, paying us no attention.

"Mom, it's me. Evangeline."

She slowly raises her head at the sound of my voice, her dull eyes lighting up when she sees me.

"Brownie," she whispers.

Brownie was her nickname for me because I was born with a head full of dark brown hair.

"I've missed you. How've you been?"

She doesn't answer. Instead, her blue eyes move to Locheran and widen. "Gargoyle," she gasps.

I glance at the guards, but they didn't hear her.

"You can see him?" I ask, and she turns her attention back to me.

"I see a man, but *he* is not human."

"How?" Locheran asks. "What are you?"

She ignores his question and takes my hands in hers. "Brownie, remember the stories I told you?"

I nod.

"My visions are coming true. They are coming for you."

"Who?"

"Here." She takes a journal out of the back of her pants and hands it over to me. "I left out details in the stories I told you because I couldn't let you stray from your destiny, but everything you need to know is in here. They want your soul so it cannot be claimed by the one who owns your heart. They want to invade his kingdom and start a war. They're evil, and they plan to kill every human they come across."

"What? Mom, I don't understand. Who is after me?"

"He will protect you. Do not leave his side."

"Who? Locheran?"

"The king. He is your mate. With you, he is stronger. With him, you are invincible."

Still holding my hands, she begins chanting in a language I don't recognize. A pain pierces through my palm, and the smell of burning skin fills the air.

Locheran makes a move to intervene. "Wait," I say.

I hold back my agony because one, I don't want the guards to interrupt and take her away, and two, I have no doubt she's doing some sort of spell meant to protect me.

"Are you okay?" Locheran asks, concerned as tears fall down my cheeks.

"Yes," I manage to croak out.

I'm seconds from pulling my hand back, no longer able to tolerate the stinging ache, before my mother stops chanting.

She looks me dead in the eyes and says, "This will give you life," before slumping over.

"Mom?" I stand, clutching my marked palm and walking to her side to shake her shoulder.

That's when the guards decide to do their job and march over to our table.

"Times up."

"We still have an hour."

"She's useless. Look at her."

One of the guards, a man in his sixties with stark white hair, waves his hand in front of her face.

"See? She does this. She won't be lucid for another couple days. Come back Wednesday."

With that, the men grab my mom by the arms and leave.

"Well, shit," Locheran says.

He takes my hand to inspect my palm.

"*Well, shit,*" he repeats. "She gave you a witch's mark."

"Excuse me?"

"Your mother's a witch."

Chapter 10 - Xander

I've been pacing along the rooftop of the Basilica of St. Patrick's Old Cathedral, texting Locheran nonstop. He's been answering me, despite being annoyed as fuck with my obsessiveness, but I don't give a shit.

It's been thirty minutes of radio silence since they arrived at the hospital. I'm seconds from testing the tether and flying there to make sure my kitten is still alive.

Then I realize I will most certainly die of an exploding heart if I fly outside the limits of my kingdom. Damn royal rules. I understand they're there to make sure the cities we protect will never be left vulnerable. In the early days, gargoyle kings who left their cities returned to them under attack.

That's when the rule was put in place.

My phone dings with a text and the tension racing through my body eases.

Locheran

> **We're done with visitation. A lot to tell you about.**

> **Kitten is fine. A little spooked, but fine.**

> **Stop pacing the rooftop and go back to your penthouse for a drink. She'll be home soon.**

Me

> **You know I don't drink anymore.**

Locheran

> **You might want to after what we have to tell you.**

Well...shit.

I call Thorne to take over command, then fly home.

When I get inside my penthouse, I shower and change into a pair of sweats and a t-shirt, then pour myself a glass of whiskey. The golden liquid burns as it goes down, and I refill the glass because my nerves are a wreck while waiting for them to return.

I lose track of time, and when the two walk through the door, I'm ten glasses deep.

Ten glasses. It used to take half that to get me wasted when I was younger.

"Kitten," I belt out, making her jump. I walk to her, arms open.

"Are you drunk?" Locheran asks, amused.

"Perhaps," I say and bring Evangeline in for a kiss. I cocoon her within my wings for privacy.

She melts into the kiss, her hands smoothing up my chest and to my neck where her fingers take hold of my hair.

I grab her ass and lift her, her short, thick legs swinging around my body.

"Do I need to leave?" Locheran asks, and I break the kiss to answer 'yes' the same time Evangeline answers 'no.'

My kitten sighs and places her head on my chest.

"We need to talk about the visit with my mother," she says and squirms in my arms. I begrudgingly release her from the cocoon and set her down.

Evangeline searches my cabinets until she finds a glass and fills it with ice water. She holds it out for me to take.

"As fun as you seem while drunk, we need you sober for this. Drink up."

I down the water, then refill the glass. My tolerance for booze isn't what it used to be, so the water works through my blood quickly, and the bliss of being drunk fades nearly immediately.

"Okay, talk," I say once we sit around the kitchen island.

"Her mother knew I wasn't human," Locheran begins. "She couldn't see my true form, but she knew I was a gargoyle."

"A seer possibly?"

"She did say her visions were coming true," Evangeline adds. "The stories she told me were premonitions about my future. She also gave me this."

She pulls a journal out of her purse.

"Everything she told me as a child but with all the details she left out."

She sets it on the counter and stares at it as if it's a snake about to attack.

"I haven't opened it yet. I couldn't. I wanted to wait and read it with you." She chews on her bottom lip. "She told me you're my mate."

"Oh?" I ask, my voice an octave higher.

"Does that mean fated mate? Like...a soulmate? Wait."

She starts pacing the kitchen.

"It all makes sense now. It's why I can see your true form, isn't it? Why I can see all the gargoyles' true forms? And this intense attraction to you? OH MY GOD."

She pauses and covers her mouth with her hand.

"Is that why your cum tastes so good?"

"That's TMI," Locheran grumbles, but Evangeline doesn't hear him and keeps rambling. She's freaking out, speaking a mile a minute. There's no way I can avoid this topic anymore.

"Also, I swear I heard you in my head. Can you hear my thoughts too?"

"If you project them to me, yes."

"So, it's true? We're fated mates?"

"Yes."

She crosses her arms. "Do I not get a choice?"

"You do. You can choose not to accept the bond."

"And, what? You die? New York City gets attacked by evil?"

"Yes," Locheran answers, and I almost murder him for real this time. "I'm just going to go."

He stands, sensing my anger.

"By the way, her mother is a witch," Locheran adds before slipping out the door.

I turn to Evangeline for an explanation, but she sits with her arms crossed, staring into the void.

"Evangeline—"

"Whatever is hunting me wants my soul so you can't claim my heart. They want to invade your kingdom and start a war. They're planning to kill every human they come across."

"This is what your mother said?"

She nods. "She envisioned this when I was just a child. She knew this day would come. My father thought she'd lost her mind, but it's all true. She's been trying to protect me my entire life. She marked my palm."

She pauses to show me, and I take her hand in mine to inspect the symbol branded on her skin. It resembles a daisy with a circle around it.

"It's a hexafoil."

"What?"

"A mark of protection. I see it mostly on buildings but rarely on humans. Though, this one is different. There's a burst of light behind it."

"Will this prevent me from being kidnapped?"

"In theory, yes. Just like the flowers you have tattooed on your body, hexafoils ward off anything that has ill intent. But in my world, there's always going to be a supernatural entity or being more powerful. Not even protection spells or objects can stop them."

"I...I don't know if I'm strong enough for this. Any of it. Being someone's fated mate...something evil wanting me dead..."

Her voice cracks and tears fill her eyes.

"Kitten," I whisper. "I will protect you, mate or not. I will not let anyone take you, even if you decide not to accept the bond. You need to follow your gut. Listen to your heart."

She scoffs.

"How do I know what's real and what's the fated mate bond?"

"Because if you didn't have any attraction or feelings for me, the bond would know, and it would weaken and eventually break. You'd no longer stand to be near me. Is that how you feel?"

"Well, no." She lets out a shuddering breath. "I'm just ...scared. I spent years in an abusive relationship. I signed up for that fucking app because I wanted something fun and casual. I didn't want to be tied down to another man. Or gargoyle."

She smiles briefly before her thoughts get the best of her.

"I'm...overwhelmed. Can we not talk about this anymore? All I want to do is snuggle on the couch with you and watch a movie."

"That sounds like the perfect way to end this night. Are you hungry? I'd love to cook for you."

Her eyes light up. "I knew you could cook."

I shrug. "I'm not bad. What do you want to eat?"

"Surprise me."

She trusts me to cook her dinner *and* choose which meal to make? I'm both honored and nervous about getting it right.

"Do you want something to drink?"

"I can get it," she says and walks to the cabinet where I keep wine glasses.

I get to work, and Evangeline moves around my kitchen as if the penthouse is already her home. *It's hers if she wants it.* She pours two glasses of wine—one for me and one for herself—then leans against the island to watch me.

"Like what you see?"

"Yes," she purrs.

"What are you going to do about it?"

She giggles. "Nothing because I'm hungry. I'll just enjoy the show."

I consider stripping to cook in the nude and *really* giving her a show, but the moment I set out the ingredients for chicken tacos, Evangeline's eyes light up with excitement.

"Tacos are my favorite!"

I wondered why I had a sudden craving for tacos.

"Are they yours too?"

My favorite food? That's a tough one. Living for one thousand years, I've come to love many meals.

"Tacos are in my top five, at least. However, I'd say coq au vin is my favorite. It's a classic French dish. It's something my mother used to make for family dinners."

"I've never had French food."

"Really?"

"My ex didn't like to try new things. What is the coq au vin dish?"

"Well, it's chicken braised with red burgundy wine. It has lardon—that's pork fat—mushrooms, and garlic."

"Aside from the mushrooms, that sounds fantastic."

I dump the chicken into a pan and season it, and while it sears, I place the shells on a plate and put toppings in bowls: cheese, sour cream, salsa, guac.

"Favorite color?" I ask while chopping the tomatoes and keeping this game of get-to-know-you going.

Her cheeks blush, and she chews on her lower lip. "Purple, but I swear I've loved that color since I was a kid. Though now it makes sense, with you being my fated mate."

I want to ravish her for that answer.

"What about you? Favorite color?"

"Brown."

"Brown? No one likes brown. Why?"

I shrug. "Maybe because it's the color of my fated mate's hair."

"Touché." She giggles and swipes a bite of tomato from the pile. "Tell me about your family."

I pause because I rarely speak about my family. My parents were never the loving type. That's how most royals are. They're all about ruling their kingdoms and staying professional, keeping their emotional attachments minimal as battles tend to take our kind to an early grave.

"Well, my father rules over Paris, and my older brother Magnus is his commander."

"You have a brother?"

"And a sister. You've actually met her," I say. "Elara is my sister."

"Wait, really?" She frowns. "Why didn't you introduce her to me as your sister?"

I pour the chopped tomatoes in a bowl and add it to the lineup.

"Elara likes to separate herself from me. She doesn't want to be known as the king's sister. The other soldiers tease her enough about it already, calling her princess. I guess I'm so used to *not* addressing her as my sister, I didn't think to introduce her to you that way."

"Oh. I guess that makes sense. Also, I don't think she likes me."

"Elara doesn't like anyone," I chuckle.

"Well, she needs to get over that. I could really use a friend. I haven't made any since moving here a few months ago. Except for my coworkers, and we're always working or too exhausted to hang out on our days off."

"Elara's not really...friend material."

"Don't worry, I'll charm her."

"I don't doubt that."

I work on my glass of wine while waiting for the chicken to finish cooking. Evangeline is already on her second glass. It's quite nice having someone to drink with, to share my life with, to cook meals for.

"How did you become king of NYC? Did your brother not want the role?"

"My brother is a warrior, not a leader. I was chosen for this role by the Council of Gargoyle Elders because while I fought in battles alongside my brother and father, I also sat in strategy meetings and shadowed my father when he made executive decisions. All my brother cared about was fucking and fighting.

"When they chose me over him, he was furious, and he challenged me to a brawl. Winner gets New York City."

"Guess you won."

"I did, and he's refused to speak to me since."

"And the Council never considered him for king of any other city? Even after all these years?"

"My father will not allow it. My brother makes rash decisions that cost lives. Elara claims he's changed over the past few decades. They're close and speak almost every day. She says my father keeps him in check. He gave him the commander title to satisfy his need for power. Seems to be working."

Evangeline takes a sip of her wine. "Wow. I'm sorry your brother's an asshole."

I laugh heartily because this human always amuses me, even when recalling tough moments of my past.

"Your turn. Tell me about your life," I say, dumping the cooked chicken in a bowl and setting it with the rest of the ingredients. "Do you have siblings?"

Her smile falters slightly.

"My mom struggled getting pregnant, so it's just me. But I still had the best childhood. At least, up until my father sent my mom away." She swishes the wine in her glass while gathering her thoughts. "He was rarely home. He worked for a company that had offices around the country, so he traveled a lot. He'd be gone for two weeks at a time. I missed him, but my mother kept me company. She was my best friend. We did everything together.

"We lived in a small town surrounded by the woods. She'd take me on hikes along the trails, and we'd walk a mile from our home. She taught me how to build a fire pit, and we'd dance around the flames. I remember her saying words in a different language. I always thought she made it up, but now I'm guessing she was chanting spells to protect me."

"So your mother is a witch with sight."

She nods, blankly staring ahead. "She knew from the day I was born that I was important...that I was your fated mate."

I also knew Evangeline was important from the moment we met.

With the tacos done, I set out two plates. That snaps her from her memories, and she moves next to me to start assembling her meal.

"I can't believe it took forty years and a shitty marriage for me to find you."

I growl at the mention of her ex, and Evangeline's cheeks warm red. "If I ever catch that man in New York City, I won't hesitate to kill him."

"I shouldn't find that sexy, but I do."

"Be careful what you say, Kitten. I've been struggling not to grab you and throw you on top of the island to have dessert before dinner."

She giggles. "You're insatiable."

"It will only get worse the more we're around each other, especially if we prolong accepting the bond."

"I want to know more about that. What does it entail?"

"Well..." I exhale a long breath because the bonding ritual is intense. I hesitate to explain it, but I suppose up until now, nothing else has scared her away. "When we make love, we must reach orgasm simultaneously. My cock will then knot, and I won't be able to remove it from your cunt until all my cum is poured inside you. I will bite you and drink your blood. My immortality will be shared with you, and once the magic is inside you, you must finish the bonding ritual by biting me and ingesting my blood."

She stops preparing her taco and stares at me, mouth open.

"I know it sounds—"

"Hot as fuck!"

Okay. She's not scared but turned on. This is good.

"I've been told it's euphoric, and we will spend days fucking to fuel and strengthen the bond."

Her eyes travel down my front to my cock. It presses against the fabric of my sweats just thinking about completing the bond ritual with her.

She tilts her head to the side, her brows furrowing.

"What did you mean by your cock will knot?"

Chapter 11 - Evangeline

“The base of your penis...expands?”

He nods.

“Is it for pleasure?”

“Yes, and to breed.”

A strange laugh bubbles up my throat and out of my mouth. “You want to have babies with me?”

“I’d be honored.”

“Does your penis knot every time we have sex?”

“Naturally, yes, but I can control it and will it not to.”

“So I won’t get pregnant the first time we have sex?”

“No. Only when you and your body are ready.”

“Oh,” I say, my voice an octave higher.

Xander’s eyes widen, clearly seeing my...panic. “Do you not want children?”

"I...um...maybe? I don't know. Brandon never wanted kids."

I chug the rest of my wine, then pour another full glass while composing my words. I did *not* expect to be talking about having kids with my failed 'one-night stand' just a few days after meeting him.

"Growing up, not having any siblings, I always dreamed about having at least two kids. Then I met Brandon, and he hated children. He convinced me I didn't want them either. I'm glad we never had any because that would have tied me to him. Now I've met you, and we're mates and..."

My gargoyle king gives me a lopsided smile.

"But I'm forty years old. I'm getting too old to have a baby."

He lifts his hand and tucks a piece of my hair behind my ear. "Remember what I said about sharing my immortality with you?"

My mouth drops open, but no words come out. Yes, I do remember him saying that, but I didn't let it sink in. How the hell are you supposed to react to someone telling you that fucking could lead to immortality?

Okay, I know there's more to it, but still.

"Yes, I suppose you did say that."

"You will stop aging. Your immune system will fortify. You can still get sick and injured; however, you will heal faster, and dying will become difficult. You will be able to survive a gunshot wound or being stabbed in the heart, unless it is a warspear that pierces it. Warspears are made of iron, which is toxic to gargoyles and their mates. And if I were to die, then you will likely pass shortly after. Losing a mate is the most painful experience."

Well, that's morbid.

"So, you're basically saying we can enjoy the honeymoon stage for a few years before deciding to have kids?"

He smiles and nods. "I like your line of thinking."

We sit on the stools at the kitchen island to eat. Birdie jumps up on the countertop, trying to convince us to share. Xander is wooed by her adorableness and feeds her some chicken.

"She likes you."

"Cats and gargoyles have been friends for centuries."

"Except for Locheran."

Xander chuckles. "He says they're evil. I think it's because one scratched him, and he was a big baby about it."

We finish our dinner and move to the living room with our glasses of wine. I select my favorite movie to watch, *Ever After*. Xander's favorite movie is *The Godfather*, which I haven't seen, so maybe we'll watch that next time.

Between my stomach being full of delicious tacos, the wine making me tipsy, and being content as fuck, I make it halfway through the movie before falling asleep.

I wake up well before the sun has set, and rush to the bathroom to relieve myself of all the wine I drank last night.

Yesterday was exhausting, to say the least. My mind is still trying to process...everything. My mother branding me and telling me I'm a target because I'm Xander's mate. Him explaining the bonding ritual. Knotting shouldn't sound hot, but I kept visualizing his cock expanding while inside me. I almost had to change my panties with how wet I got.

I return to bed to watch Xander sleep. He has a king-sized bed, which is good since he's massive. He's long and wide, and when he sleeps, he spreads out. He kicked me a couple times overnight while tossing and turning. It's the second night in a row his sleep has been riddled with bad dreams.

I can only hope once I accept the bond—which still terrifies me to think about—his restless nights will no longer be a thing.

God, he's beautiful. His long lashes flutter over his lavender cheeks. His smooth skin is flawless and always burns hot. The blue mane of hair never seems to frizz or get ratty, and I'm envious of the luscious locks.

I wonder if he'd let me braid it.

I reach out my finger and trace it down his nose to his plump, wide lips.

He's a wonderful kisser.

I lean up on my elbow and cover his mouth with mine. The moment our lips touch, his eyes shoot open, and his arm wraps around me, tugging me on top of him.

"Well, good morning, Kitten," he says, smoothing his hands up and down my thighs.

I'm now on top of his groin, so I start grinding in circles. His cock hardens beneath me, and he growls, the sound rumbling deep within his chest.

"When are you going to fuck me?" I whine.

"You think you're ready?"

"Yes. You said we can have sex without doing the bonding ritual, right?"

"We can."

"And you'll knot? I want to experience it, but you swear I won't get pregnant?"

"If you're not ready, then you will not get pregnant. I will knot and pour all my cum inside you if that's what you want."

I groan and reach down to tug at the band of his sweats. He doesn't stop me as I fish out his cock.

"Oh," I whisper the moment my palm slides down the length.

It's one thing seeing it, but *feeling* it is even better. The shaft is long, thick, and bulbous throughout. It's velvety, unlike the texture of the rest of his skin.

This cock is going to destroy me.

Xander inhales deeply. "Fuck, I love the smell of your cunt when you're turned on. You get so wet for me."

I groan and use his pre-cum as lubricant as I fist him harder, squeezing and twisting.

He closes his eyes and continues to rub his hands up and down my thighs—always needing to touch me.

"I want you inside me, Xander."

Without warning, he flips us over, my back hitting the mattress. Xander crawls between my legs and slowly peels off my pajama pants and panties, tossing them over the side of the bed.

He sinks two fingers inside me, and I arch off the mattress.

"You think you can take me?"

"Yes, Xander, please."

"So greedy, Kitten."

"I am. I need you."

I try to reach down for his cock again, but his wings swoop in and pin my hands above my head.

My new favorite thing.

"Can you be patient for me?"

"Yes. I'll be patient."

"Good girl."

The tip of his cock teases my entrance. He runs it up and down, slathering it in my pleasure.

"I'm going to go slow, okay?"

When I nod, he pushes in an inch.

"Fuck," I scream.

My pussy stretches around the bulbous tip.

"You're doing so well, Evangeline."

He slides in more, now halfway. I squirm underneath him and attempt to break free of the winged binds.

"You're being such a patient little kitten," he says and thrusts in to the hilt.

I close my eyes at the sudden tightness and try to arch off the bed again, but this time, his tail pushes on my lower stomach, holding me down.

My cunt throbs around his cock. I've never felt so full.

When I open my eyes, he's watching me. Maybe he's trying to gauge my pain.

"It feels amazing, Xander. Please start moving."

His hesitation melts away, and he pulls back, then slams back inside me. He fucks me slow at first, being ever so careful with me.

"You won't break me. Go faster, harder."

He picks up speed, his heavy balls slamming against my ass as he drives into me.

"I can feel how close you are," he groans, pumping his hips vigorously.

His hands reach up to cup my tits, squeezing and tweaking my nipples simultaneously. I moan and try to move my arms because I want nothing more than to touch him right now, but his wings will not allow it.

I've never been tied up in bed before, and not having control over what he does to my body is...freeing.

Because he's focusing on my *pleasure and worshipping every inch of* my *body.*

His tail presses against my swollen clit and starts vibrating. It only takes a few more of his thrusts before I lose it, screaming out as an orgasm ripples throughout my body.

Xander pauses, letting my pussy walls milk him.

When I'm finished, he starts moving again.

"So good, Kitten, but I'm going to need you to give me another one."

I shake my head, whimpering. "I can't."

"You can and you will."

Fuck, why was that so hot?

His tail moves in circles, massaging my clit with delicious vibrations.

Wait...that's not the only thing vibrating.

"Holy shit, Xander, is your cock vibrating?"

"Yes," he grunts, pounding into me.

The tip expands and every time he thrusts deep inside me, it brushes against my G-spot.

The vibrating—not only from his tail, but his cock—his fingers working my nipples, his wings holding me down. ..I'm already approaching another release.

"Xander, I'm going to come again."

He picks up speed at my words. Our bodies slap together, piercing the quiet of the apartment. The moment the vibration of his cock intensifies, as if he pressed a setting, I climax for a second time.

Stars dance across my vision as my body shakes through the orgasm. That's when an intense pressure, both painful and pleasant, presses against my spasming cunt.

The knotting.

His warm seed splatters my walls. I've never been able to *feel* it before.

Once Xander has emptied all his cum, he lays his head down between my breasts, catching his breath. His wings no longer hold down my arms, so I run my fingers through his sweat-matted hair. He hums at my touch.

"I need to wait until the knot goes down before I can remove myself from you. Since we are not fucking to breed, it won't take too long. Five to ten minutes maybe," he mumbles against my skin.

"How long does the knot stay...swollen when we're fucking to breed?"

"Anywhere from thirty minutes to an hour."

"Really? So your cock's just hanging out inside me until..."

He chuckles, the sound vibrating throughout my body. "Until our bodies communicate, letting us know you are with child."

He must sense my body tensing as I let his words sink in. My heart races. Though that could still be left over from the intense sex we just had.

"Like I said, it won't happen until you're ready."

He lifts his head and smiles.

"Are you okay?"

I don't tell him that my reaction to his words wasn't panic. It's more because our talk about knotting and getting pregnant didn't scare me at all. Logically, talking about this with someone I've just met should raise all the red flags and send me running.

Instead, I almost feel content. Happy. Eager for this life he paints for our future.

Our future.

"Evangeline?" he asks, worry nipping at his voice.

"I'm more than okay, my king. I'm fucking amazing."

I lean down to kiss him. His mouth hungrily devours mine, his long, thick tongue exploring every inch, as if it'll be the last time we kiss.

After we make out for at least five minutes, he finally, and carefully, pulls out of me.

"Now," he says, standing. "We're going to shower, and you're going to let me wash you."

"I am?"

"Yes. And then I'll cook you breakfast."

"You spoil me."

"Evangeline, you deserve to be treated like a queen. Washing you in the shower and making you breakfast is the bare minimum."

I take his offered hand, and he pulls me out of bed.

"I'm going to kill your ex for making you feel as if you're not worth being loved and worshiped."

The thing is, I believe he really would kill my ex, and I'm not even mad about it.

Chapter 12 - Xander

"**I**'m going, and you can't stop me."

Evangeline stands in the kitchen, dressed in scrubs, with her hands on her hips.

It's been two weeks since she found out her mother's a witch and something evil is out to kill her to end my reign. Evangeline took time off work—and I didn't even have to beg her—stating personal reasons, and we've been taking time getting to know each other.

And having a lot of sex.

She's yet to accept the bond. I don't want to rush her. It's a big decision, and her abusive marriage is the one thing keeping her from making it. Plus, it's only been two weeks. For humans, it's inconceivable to fall in love within that amount of time. They're not as open when it comes to accepting the magic and the unexplainably intense attraction that comes with the bond.

For me, I grew up dreaming about this moment. I'd been expecting it and hoping for it. I knew since the night we met that she would be my forever.

Our *need* for each other grows stronger every day, and we can barely keep our hands off each other. But it's also putting us both on edge. We fight almost as much as we fuck.

Like right now.

She wants to go back to work, but her shift begins and ends in sunlight. There will be at least an hour before and after when she is without my or Locheran's protection.

"I'm going crazy, Xander. I need to get out of the penthouse," she whines.

"Then I will take you anywhere you want to go. What about a date? A redo of the night we met. I'll take you to my favorite Italian restaurant, and we'll order everything on the menu. Then we'll go on a walk along the Hudson River. I could fly us high into the sky, and we can star gaze until the sun begins to wake."

Her anger subsides, and she walks to where I stand. I've just woken up to find Evangeline dressed in her scrubs. We had plans today to join Locheran to scour her mother's journal entries. We've spent the last couple weeks trying to decipher any clues from the stories.

She was right about it having every detail, but the journal is written in a way that makes no sense. They're riddles, and I've always *hated* riddles. Even Evangeline mentioned how they weren't the same stories her mother shared, and they couldn't provide us with any new information about the evil threatening my reign.

I'm agitated and worried. My tail must give me away because she grabs it as it flickers back and forth. She kisses the tip. Her favorite part, which gives her immense pleasure when we make love.

"I want the sun on my face," she says and pouts. "Look at how pale I am. I need vitamin D."

I hold back the joke on my tongue about giving her all the 'D' she could want because she's upset with me. Frustrated, for sure. I understand. We've barely left one another's side since the night we met. I've been hesitant to take her out of the penthouse and into public where danger lurks around every corner.

It hasn't been an issue up until this point as we've been too preoccupied exploring each other's bodies.

But she's restless.

"I'll be fine. I have the tattooed heathers. I have the hexafoil to protect me until you or Locheran or whoever you send in to watch over me arrives after the sun sets."

We'll have to pose as medical staff. Not ideal, but she threatened to leave me if I didn't let her go back to work. She didn't believe her own words. I know she doesn't want to leave me. It's not like she's a prisoner here. She knows she can leave whenever she wants. I'm merely trying to convince her to never go back to work, to let me take care of her and spoil her until the end of time. She never has to worry about money ever again.

It was the wrong thing to offer because Evangeline is an independent woman. She's no longer the wife whose ex-husband controlled every decision she made. He hated that she worked, and I don't want to be that man.

"Kitten, you never have to ask my permission for anything. I just worry, and no matter what you decide or where you plan to go, I will have someone there watching over you. If I lose you..."

"You won't."

She smooths her palms over my chest, and I snatch them to place a kiss in the middle of each one. The hexafoil glows every time I do that. She rises on her tiptoes, and I lean in to claim her soft lips. She keeps the kiss short, and I whine when she pulls away.

"My sweet king. You will not lose me."

I lift her off the ground, and she wraps her short legs around my waist. I carry her over to the island and set her on top.

"I don't like it, but you are in control here," I say and press my lips against her neck. She sighs at the burst of lust that shoots through her body, something that's been happening more frequently. It's the bond tempting us—begging us to complete it. "You are not bound by me or my rules." A kiss along her jaw. "But I do plan on having a couple of my human assistants, who help me out during daylight hours, be with you at the beginning of your shift."

I lay her back onto the counter, prepared to take her pants off, when the door opens and Locheran stops in his tracks.

"Dammit. I took a gamble not calling before showing up." He walks in and closes the door. "But now that I'm here, what's for breakfast?"

I hold up a finger, about to say Evangeline is for breakfast, but she slaps her palm over my mouth.

"Xander was just about to make breakfast burritos," she says and wiggles off the island.

"Hell yeah!" Locheran walks to the coffeemaker to start a pot of Joe.

"Make yourself at home, why don't you," I grumble and get to work, because apparently, I'm making breakfast burritos.

"Are you excited to go back to—holy shit, get this thing away from me."

Birdie has jumped onto the counter where Locheran stands making coffee and rubs up against him.

"Aww, she likes you," Evangeline says.

"This is unsanitary. Her paws walk around in her toilet."

"It's called a litter box and disinfectant is a thing."

"Cat people. I swear."

"You swear, what, Locheran?"

I chuckle at my kitten's banter with my best friend. The two have quickly become close like siblings. They remind me of the verbal fights I'd have with my own brother.

Evangeline and I have shared a lot over these past two weeks, including more stories about my childhood. I told Evangeline how I haven't seen my mother or father since the 1600s and the only communication I have with them now is through a phone call or text.

I explained that I used to be close with Magnus and Elara growing up because our parents were always busy. We relied on each other until we were forced to grow up the moment we turned eighteen and joined our father's army.

Then I was sent here to rule New York City, and we grew apart, now more like strangers than brothers and sister. Which is why I was surprised when Elara requested to join my army three years ago.

I shared a lot of my experiences living in Paris and the battles I fought. Me talking about killing evil beings with nothing but a sword or my fangs often ended with Evangeline aroused and on top of me, sinking her wet pussy down onto my cock.

She told me about growing up in a small town in Upstate New York, meeting her best friend in second grade and then her ex in high school. She went to SUNY's College of Nursing in Syracuse, and her ex went to Cornell an hour away. She talked about how he slowly lost interest in her, and she suspected he cheated.

I still plan to kill that man if he ever sets foot in this city.

I'm doing my best to undo the damage he did to her confidence and sexuality. Every day, I make sure Evangeline knows she deserves to be cherished. I not only worship her body, but that beautiful, smart mind of hers as well.

Any free moment I've had these past two weeks was spent with her.

Of course, I had royal obligations that took me away. Some nights, I'd be gone until dawn, inspecting barriers and keeping them maintained. They're becoming weaker the closer I get to my one thousandth birthday. We've had a handful of demons slip through because of this, but they were quickly caught and imprisoned.

Most of the evil we encounter every day is not strong enough to bring down my kingdom like vampires who fall to blood lust and go on killing sprees. Just a few weeks ago, the vampire queen called on us to help track down an elder vamp gone rogue. He threatened the secrecy of supernatural beings by leaving bodies drained of blood for any human to find. The queen's advisor contacted me a couple of days ago saying our services were no longer needed, meaning he's either been caught...or killed.

"I'll send Elara ahead of us once the sun sets," Locheran says, and I realize I've tuned out the conversation.

"I get to see your sister today?" Evangeline asks.

She's been dying to make friends with my sister, but Elara's been away on vacation for nearly two weeks now, visiting my parents and brother in Paris. She got back yesterday.

"She'll be helping us out at the hospital during your shift," Locheran adds.

Her eyes light up, and I can already see all the questions she's wanting to ask my sister.

Elara is going to hate it, which amuses me to no end.

Once I finish preparing the breakfast burritos, we all eat in silence, savoring the meal and fueling up on coffee. At a quarter to seven, Evangeline leaves for her overnight shift.

I stand at the windows of my penthouse, watching the sun set through the UV protective glass. It's slow and torturous and, before now, I've never cared how fast the sun faded to night.

I've been texting Josh and Gary—my human assistants—for updates ever since my kitten left. They've been answering in a timely manner, but unease refuses to leave my body. My chest aches with anxiety. As I become weaker, I grow more concerned that I won't be able to rightfully defend this city if a threat were to arise.

Evil is breathing down my neck.

When the sun's final ray disappears, Locheran bursts through my door.

"I've figured it out," he says and slams the journal down on the kitchen island. "We need to break Evangeline's mother out of the hospital."

"What are you talking about?"

He flips through the pages until reaching an entry halfway through. He taps on the paper. "The story about the woman lost in the woods, lured by the evil that wants to steal her soul. The journal says she falls in love with the sun and is saved from the darkness. I don't think it means the literal sun. When Evangeline's mother gave her the mark of protection, she told her it would give her light."

"Evangeline didn't mention her mother saying this. What does it mean?"

"I don't know, but I think that mark is going to need to be...activated or something."

"And we do that how?"

"Again, I don't know, which is why we need to break out Evangeline's mother and bring her here."

I pick up the journal and skim the words. My mind reels, but what Locheran is saying makes sense. I'm not about to question the one and only lead we have to understanding the writings of a witch and seer.

"Do it. Go now."

"I thought you'd say that. Elara should be with Evangeline now. Thorne will meet you on the hospital's roof."

We leave the penthouse and take the elevator to the building's rooftop. Locheran launches north, heading to the institution to retrieve Evangeline's mother, and I fly a few blocks away to the hospital. I land on the helipad where Thorne is waiting.

He's one of my best soldiers and intimidating as hell. He's got battle scars all over his dark purple body, including one diagonal across his face when a soul-sucking demon tried to slice him with a warspear. He was sick for months with iron poisoning.

His midnight hair is braided down to his lower back, and he's as tall as me but with more muscles, which is saying something, because I'm the biggest gargoyle king in history.

Once our human forms are intact, we take the elevator down to the emergency department on the first floor. It's a busy night and people are everywhere, running around and attending to patients.

"Do you see Evangeline? Or Elara?"

"No," Thorne grunts. "Do you sense her?"

I close my eyes. Sensing my mate when we haven't completed the bond is difficult but not impossible. That invisible string that tethers our souls constantly tugs at my heart when she's not nearby.

"I cannot sense her." I clutch my chest and fall to my knees. "I actually think I might be having a heart attack."

Thorne pulls me to my feet and sets me on a chair so as not to draw attention to ourselves.

I'm struggling to breathe.

"She's...she's gone. I think they got her."

Chapter 13 - Evangeline

The walk to the hospital isn't the same.

I stop at the cathedral, expecting to feel that strange tug in my chest, but it's not there. It had to have been Xander all those times. He'd mentioned that he stands guard on the church's roof nearly every night. It's somewhat of a headquarters for him.

Is that why I was so drawn to the location?

While there was no tug at my heart tonight—only the unease of not having Xander by my side—I do sense that something is watching me. I almost call Xander in a panic until I remember he has two of his human assistants following me.

They could at least introduce themselves so I can stop freaking out.

I make it to work with five minutes to spare and clock in for my shift. I meet with the day nurse I'm replacing for reports on patients. By the time that's done, the sun is set, and a gorgeous gargoyle enters through the emergency room doors.

My eyes widen because I always forget no one else can see them like this. Then my cheeks redden because I've only met Elara once, and I was as flustered then as I am now.

She's tall, at least six feet, and curvy with black hair, a light shade of purple skin, and silver eyes like Xander.

"Hello, human," she says as she approaches me.

"Hello, gargoyle," I counter.

"Cute."

"I know I am."

She snorts, a small smile trying to break through her grumpy fanged face. She's quick to put that tough mask back up.

Her phone rings, and she rolls her eyes before answering.

"Yeah." Pause. "Oh, I'm sorry. Yes, Your Majesty?" Pause. "Fine."

She stuffs the phone back in her tight jeans and sighs.

"There's unusual activity near the hospital, and I've been ordered to take you into hiding until the threat has been cleared."

"Oh. Okay, but wouldn't I be safest here in the hospital?"

She shrugs. "I don't question my brother's orders."

I take out my phone to text Xander, but Elara snatches it from my hand.

"No phones. They could be tracking you."

She tosses it in the trash, and I almost punch her in the face, but she has more muscles than me, so I resist the urge.

Xander is not going to be happy that I'm without a phone, especially when he can't get a hold of me. Plus, who is this "they" she's talking about, and how would they be able to track me?

Something's not adding up, but what the hell do I know about gargoyle protection and evil threats against New York City?

I ask a coworker to cover for me, then Elara leads me down a less busy hallway until we reach an exit door. She opens it and waves her hand toward the dark trash area behind the hospital.

"We probably shouldn't leave."

Not to mention, my gut is telling me something is wrong. My heart pounds against my chest, almost painfully. My fight or flight is preparing to kick in.

"My brother is out there waiting for you," she says.

I expect the words to taste sour like the day Locheran lied to me, but all I taste is the coffee I had for breakfast, so I have to believe she's telling the truth that Xander is really out there.

Besides, this is his sister. Why would she lie to me?

We exit the hospital, and I stop in my tracks.

"Brandon?" My ex-husband stands next to the back of a van, doors wide open. He looks...different. Disheveled. His light brown hair is ratted around his head, and he hasn't shaved in weeks. His brown eyes almost seem glazed over. "What the hell are you doing here? And how did you find me?"

Before he can answer, a deep voice in the shadows to my right says, "A job well done, Elara. Brandon, put her in the van."

"I'm sorry, Evangeline," Elara whispers before Brandon pistol whips me.

My vision flickers, and I fall into my ex's arms. "Why?"

"Because he promised me power," he says, his voice void of emotion.

"You fucking dick," I mumble, fading in and out of consciousness.

He drags me to the van and stuffs me inside. The last thing I see before passing out is a gargoyle who looks a lot like Xander.

I wake up in a cold, dark room that smells like mildew. Water drips from somewhere, and the only light is a dulled bulb in the middle of the low ceiling. The space is empty except for a thin, dirty mattress where I lie.

"Finally," says the same deep voice I heard before being knocked unconscious.

I scramble to my feet and teeter with dizziness from my head wound. My hands are tied in front of me, and I pull at the rope, trying to loosen it.

Not that I would have anywhere to go.

I scan the room for an exit, but there are no windows and only one door, which Brandon is currently blocking. He stands there in a zombified state.

What the hell is wrong with him?

My eyes fall to the dark corner where the voice came from, and a gargoyle emerges, stepping into the light.

"Who are you?" I ask.

"I'm Magnus."

Wait. How do I know that name? Did I hear it from Xander?

I gasp.

"You're Xander's brother?"

That's why the gargoyle looks so familiar. He has the same lavender skin tone as Xander, same hair color except shorter, and his eyes are silver. The main difference is Magnus has a long face with sharp features, and Xander has a rugged appearance with a wide jaw and sculpted cheeks. Magnus is shorter by a couple inches too.

Elara wasn't lying because her brother really was outside waiting for me—just not my king. Was Magnus the one who called and claimed there was unusual activity outside the hospital too?

"Xander's told you about me?"

I ignore his question and ask my own. "Why are you doing this?"

"Because it's time I get what I deserve, and that's New York City."

"But Xander is ki—"

"Xander has the ability to transfer his royal duties to me."

"Why would he do that?"

"Because if he refuses, I'll kill you. With no fated mate, he permanently turns to stone when he turns one thousand. Of course, him dying before giving me the throne makes things more difficult for me. Another gargoyle will be sent in his place to assume royal duties. That's why you're here, short one. He will hand me the throne to save you."

Tears fall down my cheeks, but I need to be strong. I can't let Xander down by breaking apart.

"He's your brother. He did nothing wrong. He didn't ask to be king. He was chosen. Take it up with your Council of Elders."

"My brother has been sharing all our secrets, I see."

"He tells me everything. I'm his mate."

"Yet you haven't accepted the bond. Why?"

"That's none of your business."

"Humans and their feelings," he scoffs. "When I found my fated mate, we performed the bonding ritual the next night. We were married a week later. Why deny your destiny?"

"You don't know shit about my destiny."

"That's where you're wrong. You see, my sister has been telling me everything I need to know. The visit with your mother. That mark on your palm. You being the one thing standing between me and my plan to rule New York City."

Why would Elara betray Xander? I can't think about that now. I need to keep Magnus talking. Xander is on his way, and he's close. I can *feel* him.

"You gain control over New York City and then what? What's your plan? Because I know you won't keep me and Xander alive once he transfers over his royal powers."

He chuckles and slowly paces the room.

"You're a smart human, aren't you? I can see why you're my brother's fated mate."

He stops and looks me up and down.

"How lucky he is too. If I didn't have my own wife, I'd consider keeping you for myself."

Gross.

Magnus slowly walks toward me, and I back up against the wall, closing my eyes as he enters my personal space. His finger traces along my tattoos peeking out from my scrubs, creating little lightning storms of electric currents. It's shocking him, a warning not to hurt me. If it's painful, he doesn't show it, because he hasn't stopped touching me.

"My sister told me about these. They're meant to protect you from evil, but the thing is, they're useless against humans. Lucky for us, you have an ex-husband who's a money-hungry, power-seeking twat. All we did was offer him his own law firm and a hefty paycheck to help us kidnap you."

If Xander doesn't kill Brandon, I will.

Magnus leans in and sniffs my neck. I shiver, revolted by his nearness.

"And my plan for New York City? It's time for supernatural beings to take over. *We* are at the top of the food chain. *Humans* are beneath us. I'm growing an army, short one. This is why that rogue vampire failed with his plan. He didn't have the support, the numbers. The shifters, demons, orcs, and all of the other supes around this city will switch to my side once I remind them that we're too powerful to be hiding in the shadows. It starts with New York City, then the United States, and the world."

A giggle slips past my lips.

"What's so funny, human?"

"Xander is going to kill you before any of that happens."

"He can try."

"Oh, he will."

My mate is in the hallway. He's already killed the handful of gargoyles and other supernatural beings that have been standing guard. At least, that's what the vision that crossed my thoughts just showed me.

I'm not sure if it was sent by him through the fated mate bond. He's been able to speak to me telepathically before, despite us not completing the bonding ritual.

Or maybe the vision is a power I inherited from my mother.

The door bursts open, and Xander and Locheran enter with long spear-like weapons in their hands.

"Grab her," Magnus growls, and Brandon lunges for me, clutching me by the throat and tugging me against his body, my back to his front. The sharp tip of a blade pierces the side of my neck.

"Don't move, or she's dead," Magnus says to them.

"Brother?" Xander asks, betrayal clouding his panicked face. "What are you doing? Does Father know you're here?"

Xander's eyes move to me, and he's both relieved I'm alive and furious that my mother's visions have come true.

"Father knows nothing. I'm here to take what's mine," Magnus says and gestures to Brandon, who pushes the knife in deeper. I cry out in pain, and Xander takes a step toward me. "Careful, little brother, I will have that man end her life. I don't need her for my plan."

"You don't have to do this. Tell me what you want and it's yours."

"Xander, no," I say, and Brandon covers my mouth with his palm.

"Transfer your royal powers to me. I will rule New York City, and you can have your mate and live happily ever after."

"Done," Xander says and holds out his hand.

"That easy? Are you so pussy-whipped that you'll throw your life away for a human who has yet to accept the bond?" Magnus laughs. "How sad, little brother."

He clutches Xander's hand and light shoots out from the embrace, filling the room.

It lasts barely a minute before dimming. Xander releases his grip and stumbles backwards.

"It's yours," he says weakly.

"One more thing, brother," Magnus says, smugness filling his voice. "We can't have you bonding with your mate and gaining strength to fight me for your kingdom."

A sharp pain rips through my chest. I look down to see a knife protruding from my heart.

"You stabbed me?"

"He told me I had to," Brandon says, his voice still monotone, as if he's been hypnotized.

I fall to the ground and darkness threatens to take me. Everything seems to move in slow motion, including Xander, who rips Brandon's head off his body.

My mate's agonizing roar as he takes me in his arms is the last thing I hear before I die.

Chapter 14 - Xander

I scoop Evangeline into my arms and run through the abandoned Brooklyn warehouse where my brother brought her.

Magnus is long gone, making his exit the moment I collapsed to my knees next to my mate after killing the asshole who stabbed her.

"We knew this could happen," Locheran says, running behind me. "We know how to fix it."

"I know," I growl.

Blood is everywhere, Evangeline's blood and the blood of her ex-husband. I didn't hesitate to kill him. The man had it coming, not only for how he treated Evangeline, but for all the crimes he's committed as a sleazy lawyer.

I've had a private investigator following the fucker since the moment Evangeline told me about him. I needed surveillance on him to make sure he didn't try to come back for my kitten. The investigator has also been compiling evidence of Brandon's infractions: jury and witness tampering to win cases, bribery, and money laundering. I'd planned on turning everything over to the police but killing him was far more satisfying.

The building's exit comes into view, and I extend my wings to prepare for takeoff.

"Call a cleanup crew and have them get rid of that lowlife ex, then meet me back at the penthouse," I tell Locheran and launch myself into the sky. "Stay with me, Kitten."

The flight takes less than ten minutes and when I walk through the door, Evangeline's mother is standing next to the kitchen island.

"Set her down."

I do, and Mira gets right to work.

"Your hand, gargoyle king."

I hold out the hand Mira marked after Locheran broke her out of the hospital and brought her to my penthouse. The sigil resembles an 's' with a vertical line through the middle and a burst of light behind it.

"You live a life of darkness, but she is your light. She is the sun you will worship from now until death. Her mark will bring her back to life. Your mark will save her soul."

I am the night, and Evangeline is my sun.

Mira places Evangeline's hand on top of mine, lining up our marks. Light explodes from our embrace, similar to what happened at the warehouse with my brother.

After finding out Evangeline had been kidnapped, Thorne had stumbled upon my human assistants, left for dead near the dumpsters behind the hospital. Gary, who was barely conscious, managed to tell us they were attacked after dropping off Evangeline for her shift. They caught Elara and a gargoyle who looked a lot like me putting her inside the back of a van in an alleyway behind the hospital.

A gargoyle who looked like me? It had to be Magnus.

When Mira arrived, she used the tracking spell she laced throughout Evangeline's hexafoil to pinpoint her location inside a warehouse in Red Hook.

Then she gave me my own mark, which was supposed to incapacitate Magnus so I could save Evangeline. Once she was safe and my brother captured, I had planned to hold him in a jail cell in the basement of Saint Basilica's and let the Council of Gargoyle Elders decide what to do with him.

Magnus was stronger than we anticipated. Now he believes I've given him my royal powers over New York City. He'll be furious once he finds out he doesn't have the throne. He will fight to the death to claim it.

"You are giving her part of your life. You are the reason she will live," Mira says, pulling me from my thoughts.

I can *feel* the energy coursing through my body and pouring into my mate.

"Speak to her. Convince her to come back."

I palm her cheek with my free hand.

"Kitten, please," I begin, tears claiming my voice. "You are the best thing to happen to me in all of my 999 years. You are the sun that doesn't turn me to stone. You own my heart. You've had it since the first message on that damn dating app. Come back and let me cherish you the way you deserve. I love you."

Evangeline gasps, and her body arches off the countertop. Her eyes pop open, and I release her hand.

"Kitten," I whisper, lifting her off the island and cradling her in my arms. "Are you okay? How do you feel?"

"Like I was stabbed in the heart," she mumbles, and I let out a bark of laughter.

She nearly dies, and she's telling jokes? God, she's perfect.

"I need water," she croaks.

"I'll get it," Mira says, and Evangeline jerks her head to the sound of her mother's voice.

"Mom?"

"Yes, Brownie, I'm here."

"I don't understand."

"I broke her out of the hospital," Locheran says, entering the penthouse with Thorne behind him.

"How?" Evangeline asks.

Locheran shrugs. "Easy. I showed them some fake credentials and told them we were moving her to a hospital here in Manhattan. I also forged your father's signature to name you as your mother's proxy. That way, you can release her to herself if you want."

"And you just happen to have fake credentials lying around?" Evangeline asks with a snort.

"Of course." Locheran shrugs. "Most supernaturals have many fake credentials *and* documents."

Evangeline squirms in my arms, and I reluctantly let her down. She hugs Locheran first, and he stills because I don't think I've ever seen anyone hug the gargoyle before. At least, not in a friendly sense.

I don't think *I've* ever hugged my best friend.

"Thank you, Commander," Evangeline whispers.

She turns to her mother once she releases Locheran. Mira hands her the glass of water, but Evangeline sets it on the counter to embrace the woman.

"I'm never letting you go back to that place. I should have fought Dad to have you released sooner. I'm sorry."

"Don't be sorry, Brownie," her mother says, rubbing her back. "You were not in a place to worry about my troubles. I'm just happy you finally got out of that abusive relationship."

Evangeline pulls away, her face scrunched in confusion. "Did you know about Brandon? I mean, did you have a vision that I'd be with him?"

"No, dear," the witch says, pushing back a piece of her daughter's hair. "I cannot control my visions. The ones concerning you have always been about the supernatural evil threatening your life. Unfortunately, that did not include evil humans."

Evangeline gasps. "Oh, Xander. You transferred your royal power to Magnus."

She has yet to take a drink of water so I place the glass in her hand. While she rehydrates, I explain the decoy mark her mother gave me to trick Magnus into believing he's now the king of New York City.

"Once he discovers the truth, which he might already have, he will seek me out to challenge me. He will fight for the throne."

"Do you really have a throne?" Evangeline asks, her eyes lighting up.

"No, but if you want one, I shall buy it for you."

She giggles. "Always spoiling me."

"And you should let me."

Her smile drops, and she sits down on a stool.

"You killed my ex. I saw you rip his head off," she whispers, more so in awe than fear or anger. "Brandon wasn't himself. He seemed out of it."

"A compulsion spell," Mira explains. "Magnus might have found a witch to help him."

"He promised Brandon power," Evangeline continues. "His own law firm and money. Could he do all that?"

"He could have," I begin, "but knowing Magnus, he would have killed Brandon after he was done using him."

Evangeline nods blankly. After the night she's had, I expect her body will soon be claimed by exhaustion.

I turn to Thorne, who's been leaning against the door, arms crossed. "Please take Mira to a guest apartment. Make sure she has everything she needs for the night. Clean clothes, toiletries and such."

He nods, and I turn to Mira.

"Thank you for everything tonight. My soldier, Thorne, will take care of you."

Mira places her palm on my forearm, and I suck in a sharp breath. Whatever spell she just zapped into my body instantly calmed my frayed nerves.

"Sleep well, king. Tomorrow, my daughter will be ready to hand over her soul to you."

My eyes widen.

Evangeline will want to complete the bonding ritual tomorrow? It's a day I've been waiting for since we met.

Mira gives me two reassuring pats, then walks to Thorne. He opens the door and holds out his arm for the witch to take.

Once they're gone, Locheran turns to me.

"Guess that's my cue to leave too." He slaps a clawed hand on my shoulder. "You and your kitten take a few days off. I got things handled. I'll form a battle plan. If anything dire arises, I'll come find you."

I bring my best friend and commander into a hug, something I vow to do more. All my life, he was a better brother than Magnus. Locheran's unsure what to do at first before his body relaxes, and he accepts the embrace.

"I owe you, brother."

Locheran clears his throat. "I'll take you up on that someday," he says, and we part.

The moment he leaves, I pick Evangeline up to carry her into the bedroom.

"How many apartments do you own in this building?"

"I own all the units on the two floors below the penthouse," I explain while stripping her out of her bloodied scrubs. "A few of my soldiers stay in some of them to be near me. I always keep a few apartments vacant in case of emergencies like tonight. Your mother will be staying in one."

"It'll be safe, right?"

"I have no doubt your mother will add her own wards, but yes, it will be safe."

I lead her to the bathroom where I wash her body and hair then dry her off with a towel. I dress her in a pair of her pajamas and lead her back into the bedroom where I tuck her in.

Birdie jumps on the bed and curls up by her side.

"My kitten and her cat," I say.

Evangeline hums. "Thank you for bringing me back to life. Dying wasn't fun. It was like I was stuck in a dark room, yelling loud enough that I lost my voice. No one could hear me. Then I saw a light, and I heard your voice."

I settle in behind her, draping my arm over her stomach and kissing her neck.

"Xander?"

"Yes, Kitten?"

"You also own my heart," she says.

"I do?"

"Always," she whispers and just before she falls asleep, she adds, "I love you."

Chapter 15 - Evangeline

I stand on the rooftop of Xander's building. Evil gargoyles soar over the skyline of Manhattan, reminding me of that scene from *The Wizard of Oz* when the Wicked Witch of the West sends the flying monkeys to kidnap Dorothy.

Two gargoyles swoop down, grabbing me by the arms and holding me in place. Magnus lands in front of me and stabs me in the heart.

I jerk awake, gasping for air.

It was just a dream.

I glance over at Xander, but his snores are as loud as ever. How I'm able to sleep through the sawing of logs, I'll never know.

I pick up my phone to check the time. Two more hours until sunset. There's no way I'll be able to fall back asleep. My heart rate is still high from the nightmare.

I get out of bed and use the restroom, then head to the kitchen to start up a pot of coffee. While making myself a bowl of cereal, Birdie jumps on the counter and chirps until I give her some wet food.

I finish my coffee and cereal before Xander wakes so I brush my teeth and return to bed.

I'm *ready.*

I straddle Xander, and his eyes pop open.

"Good morning, my king," I say with a smile.

"Good morning, Kitten," he echoes, smoothing his palms up and down my bare legs.

He closes his eyes when I start moving in circles over his groin.

He loves when I do this.

"I want you to claim me, Xander," I say, grinding my hips faster.

His tail snakes around my waist until the tip slips behind the band of my shorts, down to my already soaked cunt. The bulbous end presses against my clit and vibrates. I jerk at the sudden sensation.

"Are you sure you're ready, Kitten?"

"Yes, please," I gasp as Xander takes my aching nipples between his fingers. He pinches them through the thin fabric of my tank top.

The end of his tail bears down harder on my clit, the vibration turning up a notch.

Xander is still on his back, but that doesn't stop his wings from expanding. I reach out to touch them, and the moment my fingers skim over the silky membrane, he bucks. His large cock grows hard beneath me.

"You're close, aren't you?"

I nod.

"I know because I can smell that sweet cunt. Will you come for me?"

I whimper and nod again.

Xander sits up and rips my top off, allowing him to take my nipple into his mouth. His tongue lashes over the sensitive peak while his fingers tweak and pull at the other.

"Now, Evangeline, come," he says at the same time the vibrating tail intensifies, pulling an orgasm from me.

I come so hard; I see stars.

Xander doesn't give me time to recover, and he's flipping me over onto my back.

He slides off my shorts and thrusts his long, thick tongue inside me.

"Fuck, Xander," I scream and grab his horns to pull him closer.

His tongue pistons into me, and his vibrating tail returns to my sensitive clit.

I cry out, tears falling down my cheeks, as pleasure overwhelms me.

Xander builds me up, my entire body shivering with anticipation. I'm seconds from climax when he suddenly stops and removes his tongue.

"No!"

"Be patient, Kitten. I'll make sure you get another orgasm."

He slaps my aching clit, and I groan at the pain-infused ecstasy.

"Good girl. I'm going to finger your ass now. Is that okay?"

"Yes, please."

He slides a finger inside my pussy. Once it's well lubricated, he pushes it past the outer ring of my asshole. He waits for me to adjust, then pushes it in more.

When he gets down to the last knuckle, he withdraws it and adds a second one.

I suck in a sharp breath because he only has four fingers and they're all...girthy.

"Good?"

"Yes, God, keep going."

"I'm not your God, Evangeline. I am your *mate*."

He stretches me and it's a strange feeling, slightly painful, but it quickly turns to pleasure as he pumps the fingers in and out. He spits on them a few times to make sure I'm properly lubricated.

Fuck. Why is him spitting so hot?

His mouth returns to my pussy, and he's driving his tongue into me again. He finds a rhythm between finger-fucking my ass and tonguing my cunt.

I smooth my hand over his wings again, and he groans. So, I keep doing it and it's as if *my* pleasure merges with *his*. My strokes match the movement of his fingers and tongue, and it doesn't take long before another orgasm washes over me.

He moves from between my legs, crawling up my body so he can kiss me, long and hard. I taste myself as he plunges his tongue past my lips.

Nectar.

"Are you ready?" he says against my mouth.

"I'm ready."

He removes his t-shirt and sweats, his hard cock springing up the moment it's free.

He fists it up and down, letting the pre-cum lubricate the shaft.

Not that he needs it; I'm soaked.

He presses the tip to my opening.

"Remember, we will reach orgasm at the same time. My cock will knot, and I will bite you while all my cum empties inside you. Then you finish the bonding ritual by biting me. You have to drink my blood. You're going to be ravenous, and you won't want to stop, but you must, otherwise taking too much could make you sick. You'll know when you've had enough."

The thought of drinking blood should make me sick to my stomach, but instead, I squirm with thirst.

"I'm ready," I repeat.

Xander thrusts into me.

"It's going to happen fast, because our bodies are more than ready to unite our souls."

My moan sounds more like a scream as he hammers into me, hard enough that I hope my pussy will be bruised and battered tomorrow. His large, heavy balls slap against my ass, offering a pleasant slap of pain.

I feel the tip of his cock expand, hitting my G-spot with every deep thrust, and my walls pulse around him.

I'm close.

He picks me up off the bed and sits down so I can straddle him.

"Ride me," he growls, and he knows how much I love it when he growls.

It motivates me to move my hips, bouncing on his cock, up and down.

He cups my ass in both hands and squeezes, his claws biting into my meaty cheeks.

"I'm close," he says.

"Me too."

The base of his dick grows until he's unable to pull back out of me. I feel full with him seated inside me, the tip of his cock pressing against my G-spot.

"Xander, I'm... I'm..."

He grunts, and his wings cocoon around me.

I'm sent over the edge the moment his fangs pierce the skin between my neck and shoulder. He lets out an animalistic roar as he empties his cum inside me. An invigorating current races through my veins. Ecstasy pours into my body, the feeling so intense, I don't even register the pain from his bite as he drinks my blood like a starving vampire.

I don't know how long this lasts, but as soon as Xander retracts his fangs, I realize it's my turn.

I don't have sharp fangs to pierce his skin, so I bite down on the crook of his neck as hard as I can. A warm, savory liquid explodes into my mouth.

"That's it, Kitten, drink."

His cock is still inside me, and it *throbs* as I draw his blood into my mouth. Immense euphoria spreads like wildfire across my skin with every drop I take. It's making me *feral*. I growl and moan and claw at his back, scratching hard enough to break skin. If it hurts, he shows no sign of pain.

I feel full, but I keep drinking. It's addicting. My hunger for his blood seems like it will never end and the more I consume, the more aroused I become.

But my need to come overshadows the thirst and that's when I know it's time to stop. I remove my mouth and gasp for air.

Xander wraps his tail around my neck and squeezes. I throw my head back to scream as my cunt pulses with another orgasm. Xander joins me, pouring more cum inside me.

We lie there, huffing and puffing and bleeding all over Xander's silver sheets. After five minutes, once we've finally caught our breath, he carefully removes himself and collapses on the bed next to me.

"So good, Kitten," he says and tugs me to his side, kissing the top of my head.

"That's it? We're bonded?"

"We are. Do you feel different?"

My body vibrates, a low hum cycling through my blood. It's as if I've been underwater my entire life, and I'm now able to breathe.

A lifetime of worries, pain, and heartache...gone.

"I do feel different. I feel *alive*."

Chapter 16 - Xander

Evangeline and I spend the next few days in bed, giving ourselves to each other until our bodies could no longer physically function. We'd sleep then wake and fuck, then shower and eat and fuck some more. It was a beautiful cycle, one that is coming to an end now that the fated mate bond has been satiated.

Locheran has been keeping me updated on battle plans. He said there's been no sightings of Magnus. When I do find him, the Council of Gargoyle Elders has given me permission to end his life for violating the most coveted law of our kind.

Do no harm to gargoyles or their potential and bonded mates.

Elara is in custody after turning herself in and confessing everything. She said Magnus forced her to help him and threatened to kill her fated mate if she refused. I'll let the Elders and my parents decide what to do with her.

"So basically, sex saved his life," Locheran says as we sit around the dining room table having dinner.

Mira declined our invitation saying she's still not used to socializing after all her years in the psychiatric hospital. Evangeline was worried about her being lonely, so Birdie has been staying with the witch in one of my guest apartments in the building for the past few days. It worked out perfectly because we've been a bit too preoccupied lately to worry about taking care of anyone or anything besides ourselves.

"My pussy saved his life," Evangeline giggles.

Okay, I clearly missed a lot of their conversation.

"I've been wondering," Evangeline begins, "that night we met, how did you not know it was your brother who breached the barrier?"

I fist my hands on the table. "The asshole likely had a cloaking spell from a witch, or he could have masked his scent with one from another creature."

Evangeline nods while considering this explanation. "I can't believe the big evil hunting me my entire life was your brother."

"Actually," Locheran says, holding up a clawed finger, "I asked your mother about this. There have been many evil beings hunting you since the day you were born, all of them aiming to get rid of Xander so they could claim New York City. Magnus was the only one to succeed at kidnapping you."

"Yet he failed at the rest of his plan," I seethe, still furious he hasn't been caught.

"That reminds me," Evangeline says. "Magnus said something about a vampire's failed plan. What did he mean?"

"A rogue vampire recently went on a killing spree," I begin. "His plan was to out our kind and rule over the human world."

"Just like Magnus," Evangeline hums.

"Yep," I agree.

"Speaking of plans...what are we doing for the big one-oh-oh-oh, Xanny?" Locheran asks with a mouthful of coq au vin.

Evangeline begged me to make her my favorite meal. She's devouring it, and pride swells in my chest. She loves a lot of the things I love, like gritty crime documentaries and reality TV shows.

It's a guilty pleasure. They're fun to watch. Humans are so ridiculous.

I pause with a forkful of food halfway to my mouth, and I realize I haven't thought about how I'd celebrate my birthday because I convinced myself I wouldn't live to see it.

I was preparing myself to die.

Evangeline must see the anguish on my face, or she likely *feels* my despair now that we're bonded. She understands that I had lost hope and forgot to plan a simple celebration. She places her palm on my forearm and a wave of calm courses through my body.

Evangeline can naturally calm anyone she touches. It's a little trick she inherited from her mother.

I asked Mira why I couldn't sense this magic the night Evangeline and I met. The witch said it's such a minor power that no supernatural being would have been able to detect it. She also believes the ability was dormant, and *I* was the one to wake it up.

As if the magic within my own body called to Evangeline's.

Mira also warned us that her daughter may have other gifts emerge over the next few decades, activated by the mystical force of the fated mate bond.

I'm eager to uncover them.

"Why don't we plan a rooftop party?" Evangeline says, her voice bringing me back to the present.

"In October?" Locheran asks, scrunching up his nose.

"It might be a little chilly on October 25th, but as you know, *Locheran*, gargoyles don't get cold."

My best friend rolls his eyes at me.

"Besides," Evangeline adds. "We could get those portable heaters for the humans, which would be me and maybe my bestie, Farrah. And I bet my mom would come too! It'll be a personal and chill party. We could have barbecue, play some music and dance, and maybe we can get a projector up there and watch *The Godfather*."

A smile tugs at my lips. She remembered my favorite movie. Of course she did.

"I love this idea," I say.

"Damn. So no strippers?" Locheran whines. "What about a nightclub at least? We could rent out the place and dance and get wasted off top shelf liquor."

Evangeline snorts, not even phased by the man child gargoyle commander.

"When it's your 1,000th birthday," she says, "we'll do all those things, Loch."

"Well, start planning. My birthday is January 10th."

One second, we're laughing and the next, an explosion rips through my living room. I'm knocked to the ground a few feet away. I push debris off me, violently coughing after inhaling clouds of dust. My ears ring, mixed with the muffled wail of the building's fire alarm.

"Evangeline!"

Splinters of glass and wood embed in my palms as I crawl around on the ground, searching for my mate.

"Xander? Where are you?" her tiny voice croaks out, followed by a cough.

I use the bond to locate her amid the smoke-filled room and find her underneath part of a collapsed wall.

I lift it as if it weighs nothing.

"Are you hurt?" I ask, scanning her body.

"I have a cut on my head, and I think my leg is broken."

I help her stand, and she hisses when she tries to take a step.

"Yeah. Definitely broken."

I scoop her up in my arms. "It'll heal within a day."

"Really? Oh, right. The bond."

"Yes, you will heal from injuries faster now, just like gargoyles."

I move through the ruined dining nook into the kitchen and clear the island of debris before setting her down.

"Well, hello, little brother."

The sound of Magnus's voice has me moving in front of Evangeline to shield her.

He stands just inside the penthouse, where a massive hole replaces the wall of windows. The wind whips his long hair around his face. Behind him outside, dozens of creatures hover: gargoyles, a rogue angel, a handful of harpies, and I think I see a griffin too.

He's acquired a small but mighty army.

Mine is mightier.

My soldiers can sense my alarm, and they are already gathering to implement Locheran's battle plan. My commander still hasn't emerged from the debris and worry nips at my nerves.

"I'll go find him," Evangeline whispers.

I must have unknowingly broadcast my thoughts to her. It's a part of the bond I'm not yet used to.

"No. Stay here so I can protect you."

She slides off the island, avoiding putting pressure on her injured leg. I want to hold her, steal her away, but I can't take my eyes off my brother.

"You handle this. Let me find Locheran."

"Your leg–"

"It's fine. I'll use whatever I can find along the way as crutches."

She hobbles away before I can argue.

I slowly walk into what used to be the living room, now a pile of debris. I'm surprised the floor hasn't collapsed yet.

Police and fire sirens sound from a distance. Some of my soldiers should be there ready to intercept the first responders to stop them from coming up here.

They'll also need to do damage control on the ground. I doubt Magnus and his small army are masked. He *wants* our kind to be discovered.

"Brave of you to show your face here after attempting to kill my mate."

"You mean after a human attempted to kill your mate?" He tosses up his hands. "I'm innocent."

He smiles wide enough to show off his fangs, the cocky bastard.

"You, however, owe me a kingdom."

"I don't owe you shit."

He paces casually, his hands behind his back.

"How did you fake the transfer of power? Was it your mate's witch mother?"

I shrug.

"That's fine, Xander. My soldiers will find her. They're already in your building. I could use another witch to do my bidding."

I vaguely hear Evangeline behind me, searching the debris. She's yelling Locheran's name, but her voice is nearly swallowed by the wind filtering into the penthouse sixty floors above ground.

I mentally check in with her, making sure she's staying off her broken leg. When she assures me she's fine, I walk further into the destroyed living room toward a long, narrow cabinet where I keep one of my warspears hidden. I hope it's still locked in place and not lost in the destruction.

"What I still haven't figured out is why you're doing this. You have a coveted role as father's second. You are heir to the Paris throne. He's got to be, what, a few hundred years from retirement?"

My brother scoffs, his wings expanding, and he fists his hands at his side. He's preparing to fight.

When I finally get to the spot where I've hidden my weapon, I reveal my own wings. It blocks his view, and I use my tail to extract the warspear.

"Father won't allow me to rule Paris and you know it. I may be first born, but too much responsibility was put on me as a child. I grew up too fast and rebelled. I was young and stupid, but I learned my lesson. I changed, yet he doesn't care. He will always see me as a fuck up."

I got him, I hear Evangeline say in my head.

I answer back.

Tell him to take you to your mother. He must protect the both of you until this is over. Magnus wants to kidnap Mira for her powers.

Before she can answer, Magnus lunges for me. I move out of the way just in time, and he falls into a pile of glass and wood.

The battle begins.

I send the silent command for my soldiers to fight, and chaos erupts outside. Gargoyles collide with Magnus's army. My soldiers are carrying weapons to maim and kill: battle axes, spears, swords, and war scythes, to name a few. Some of my soldiers use their fangs to tear holes into throats while others slice open stomachs with their claws.

My attention turns back to my brother.

He's holding his own warspear now.

"What's more important, little brother? Killing me or saving your mate?"

Another explosion blows down the front door of the penthouse and a gargoyle who I recognize as one of my father's soldiers enters, dragging Evangeline in by the neck.

Traitor.

"No!"

I move to kill this asshole, but Magnus tsks at me.

"Take one more step, and he will end her life."

A roar erupts from my chest, and I hurl the warspear at my brother. He dodges it, and I use the diversion to run for him, grabbing him by the neck and catapulting us outside like a cannonball.

We thrash our wings to keep us airborne as we brawl. He uses his tail to try and stab me with his warspear, but I'm stronger now that I've mated with Evangeline. *I'm faster.* He misses with every jab, allowing me to pummel his face with punches, and I don't hold back. I hit him square in the nose, and blood pours out. I extract my claws and slice them down his chest, peeling open his marble-like skin.

All he does is laugh.

"These injuries will be healed before the night is over."

His knee makes contact with my groin, forcing me to let go as I lean over in pain. I fall a few feet in the air before I manage to compose myself.

The small distraction is all Magnus needs to grab Evangeline from my father's traitorous soldier.

"Now you have to make a choice, Xander. Hand over your royal duties to me, or your mate gets stabbed in the heart."

Magnus wraps his hand around her neck and holds her out as if he's about to drop her to the ground. She frantically claws at his arms as her air supply is slowly cut off.

"What will it be, little brother? Make your choice fast or I'll stab her with my warspear and drop her to the ground."

"I'm afraid you're done, Magnus. You've lost."

He laughs like a maniac.

"Did you not hear me? I said I'll drop her—"

"Now, Evangeline!"

She takes her palm with the hexafoil mark and slams it into his chest. Light pours into his heart and spreads over his body.

This will give you light.

The mark of protection not only brought Evangeline back to life, but it gave her the power of the sun. She can use it as a weapon, permanently turning any rogue gargoyle to stone.

We've yet to discover how she can use this against other evil beings.

What we do know is my kitten is powerful, and I'm eager to have her fight by my side as my queen.

If only she had wings.

But she doesn't, and the moment my brother's body petrifies, Evangeline falls with his solidified form.

I dive towards her like a speeding bullet and reach her halfway down the building.

I tuck her to my body, and she buries her face into my chest.

"Am I dead?"

I chuckle. "No, Kitten. I've got you. I'm so proud of you. Fuck, you were brave."

"I never knew how much I needed your praise until now."

I fly us back up to the destroyed penthouse. The battle is all but over. Magnus's army was no match for my soldiers. I sent in hundreds and had thousands more on standby.

Locheran stands just inside the debris of the living room, holding his head.

"Sorry, boss. They ambushed us."

"I'm just glad you're okay."

"Have you checked on my mom and Birdie?" Evangeline asks.

"I just got a text from Thorne," Locheran says, holding up his phone. "They're both good. Magnus and his soldiers weren't able to find her. She had a very powerful cloaking ward up around the apartment."

"Thank goodness," Evangeline says, breathing out a sigh of relief.

"Locheran, check with the soldiers on the ground. Make sure they don't need help cleaning up this mess."

The battle was masked, but it's possible some humans witnessed the beginning of the fight. We have a process of questioning humans who stumble upon our existence. We assess their reaction and decide whether to confirm what they saw—for the believers of the strange and unusual—or delude them.

The mind is a tricky thing. Most people can blame unexplained occurrences on exhaustion or simply not wanting to admit they saw something strange and unusual because no one will believe them. The skeptics will always find any explanation other than the truth.

"You got it. What are you two about to do?"

"I need to make love to my mate since I almost lost her again."

"You know you weren't going to lose me," she giggles.

It's true. We had a plan in place in case Magnus attacked. Evangeline's mother taught her how to communicate with the protection spells marking her body. She was able to essentially pause the magic of the heather tattoos and the hexafoil, which allowed Magnus and his soldiers to grab her.

He was so consumed by his need for power, he didn't realize he shouldn't have been able to touch her in the first place.

"Where are we going to make love? The penthouse is destroyed."

I lean in and kiss her gently.

"Tonight? The sky is our bedroom."

Chapter 17 - Evangeline

"What do you mean, the sky is our bedroom?" I ask and laugh nervously.

Xander holds me tighter and shoots up into the air. I scream, not expecting to be launched like a firework, and cling to him just as I did the first night we met.

He takes us above the clouds, the blanket of white giving us privacy.

"I've wanted to fuck you mid-air since the night we met."

Holy shit. We're going to have sky sex.

"Are you scared?"

I glance around and expect fear to consume me. Instead, adrenaline and excitement course through my body.

"You know what? I'm not scared. Not anymore."

It might have something to do with being nearly in-destructible now. Or maybe it's because I know Xander won't let me fall. He'll protect me.

"Good girl. Now, I want you to keep your eyes on me, okay, Kitten?"

I nod and he adjusts me so I can wrap my legs around his torso. His wings flap casually, keeping us stationary.

I'm wearing leggings, and he extracts a claw to rip the crotch to shreds.

Easy access.

"No panties?" he asks after pushing a finger past my pussy lips and sinking the digit inside me until it's down to the last knuckle. I throw back my head and moan.

"Cry out as loud as you want, Evangeline. No one will hear us up here."

He removes his finger and presses the tip of his cock at my opening, rubbing it through my pleasure.

"So wet for me. Are you ready?"

I clutch his neck harder and nod.

He thrusts up into me to the hilt, and I scream.

His hands fall to my hips, and he uses his gargoyle strength to hold me in place as his bulbous cock pounds in and out of me.

"Harder, Xander, I need more."

"You want more?" he asks, amusement filling his voice. "I can give you more."

His tail snakes around my backside and the tip presses at my puckered hole.

Xander pauses his thrusts.

"We've been stretching you out. Do you think you can take my tail while I fill your cunt with my cock?"

"Yes," I groan and squirm in his arms.

"That's a good girl. My tail's end is going to transform into a phallic shape. It self-lubricates so it can slide into you better, okay?"

No fucking way.

He doesn't let me respond before the dick-shaped end of his tail enters me. I arch my back at the sensation. The tail pulls out then thrusts back in.

I've never felt so full.

Xander finds a rhythm. His cock driving into me in tandem with his tail, both vibrating at their highest strength.

That sends me over the edge, but my king isn't being patient and keeps fucking me through the orgasm.

"I want four more tonight. Can you do that for me, Kitten?"

"Yes," I groan, and he moves one hand between our bodies and presses down on my clit.

I clutch his neck hard enough that my nails dig into his skin. I don't know how he's able to keep me held in place with just one arm. Despite knowing I could survive the fall; I'd rather not plummet to the ground. But my fears fade the longer Xander massages my clit, quickly pulling orgasm number two from me.

"Three more."

And I give him three more. One when his mouth teases my taut nipples while he fucks my cunt and ass. Another when he lifts me to his face so he can eat me out. The fifth and final orgasm hits when he fucks me until his cock knots, and he pours all his cum inside me.

"If sky sex means five orgasms, we're going to need to do this more often," I say, trying to catch my breath.

Xander is still inside me as he leisurely flaps his wings to keep us stationary in the air.

"Maybe once a month?" Xander asks.

"Or once a week."

"Every night?"

"I like your thinking," I laugh. "I do have a question though."

Xander wipes a piece of sweaty hair off my forehead. "Yes, my love."

"What happens when you remove yourself from me?"

"What do you mean?"

"Um… well… since moving to NYC, I've been shit on by a bird twice while walking down the sidewalk. Was that really a bird or gargoyle cum that fell during sky sex?"

My king bursts into a fit of laughter, his entire body shaking.

"I'm serious!"

"I know you are, and I assure you, in this instance, all my cum stays inside your cunt. That's what the knot is for."

Okay. That makes me feel better.

"Wait, what do you mean in this instance?"

"Well, not every gargoyle knots during sex. There have been a few…incidents in the past, which is why 'sky sex,' as you like to call it, is highly frowned upon."

"Did you break your own rules, Your Majesty?"

He chuckles.

"Maybe."

"So, where are we sleeping tonight?"

He starts flying…still inside me, and I'm already getting turned on again.

"We could stay in one of the apartments in my building, but I do own other apartments around the city. Your choice. I'm not tired, and I can already feel you getting worked up again."

I blush, because I'm barely able to hold back my whimpers as his entire body vibrates while flying.

"You're right. I'm not tired either. Will you fuck me all night until the sun wakes? Please, sir."

"There's my naughty kitten."

Epilogue - Evangeline
1 Year Later

It's been a year since I killed Magnus.

The day after I permanently turned him to stone, the Council of Gargoyle Elders arrived and took his petrified form back to Paris—it surprisingly didn't shatter to a million pieces after falling to the ground. Thankfully, the area below had been evacuated by Xander's soldiers during the battle.

Elara was also sent back to Paris and put on trial. She was cleared after a seer was brought in to seek her truth. They discovered Magnus had kidnapped her fated mate three years ago and had been holding her captive for years while he formed his plan to steal the throne from Xander. Elara had no choice but to help him, and he used her as a spy, forcing her to request to be put in Xander's army.

She still has to be monitored, and she's now serving in her father's army, where he can watch her as well. Her fated mate was also saved from captivity after one of Magnus's captured soldiers was tortured for information on her whereabouts.

My father discovered my mother was released from the hospital and fought to recommit her. He argued that he never gave me power of attorney, but with his signature on the papers, he was unable to prove otherwise, and a judge ruled in my favor.

He confronted me after we left the courtroom. He demanded I tell him how I did it. I claimed it was all his idea. We went back and forth for a few minutes before he accused me of being 'just as crazy as your mother.'

Guess I am.

Xander and I bought my mother a house in the suburbs where she lives with Birdie—who I visit as much as possible. Mom spends her days gardening, practicing spells, or just enjoying a life of freedom.

We meet for dinner once a week, too, where she shares more stories that have me wondering if they're ones she made up or visions of mine and Xander's future.

My favorite is the story of the half-gargoyle, half-human prince who grows up to be a warrior and takes over an expansive kingdom when his father decides to retire.

Xander will be able to travel the world when he hands over the throne to our child.

Not that we're pregnant. I'm not. We still haven't decided when to have kids. We're enjoying each other too much right now.

Plus, today is our wedding day.

"Do gargoyles get old?" I ask, putting on my makeup.

We decided to keep the wedding small and nontraditional. No church, no white dress, and no believing the superstition that it's bad luck for the groom and bride to see each other before the wedding.

I wanted to get ready in the same room as my future husband and spend every last second of my old life with him before becoming Evangeline Basque.

"Of course we do. I'm 1,000 years old."

"No, I mean like old and wrinkled, gray hairs and shit."

He chuckles as he buttons up his shirt.

"Gargoyles who reach five digits get wrinkles and gray hair."

My mouth drops open.

"There are gargoyles who are 10,000 years old?!"

"My grandfather, who is head of the Council of Gargoyle Elders, is one of them. He's 12,436 to be exact. He once protected early civilizations in Turkey."

"Holy shit. That's...old. But fascinating! I'd love to meet him. Your father too. I really hate the rule that tethers you to New York City."

He gives himself one more glance in the mirror and turns to me.

My handsome king. He wears a simple black dress shirt and pants paired with a black buckle and shoes.

I'm wearing a pastel yellow sundress. My hair is piled up in a messy updo.

He is the night, and I am the sun.

Since I'm still technically human, I'm able to go out during the day, but our wedding is being held a few minutes after sunset on the rooftop of our apartment building—the one damaged during the battle that Xander and his soldiers spent months rebuilding.

"Ready?" I ask, reaching for my king.

Even with heels, I'm nowhere near as tall as him. My head barely reaches his chest, forcing him to lean down to kiss me.

"Ready."

The ceremony will be quick and simple, because everything else in our lives has been complicated. Xander walks me down the aisle, since my father is no longer in my life. The guest list is small. My mother and my bestie Farrah—who thinks I'm getting married to another human—and about a dozen of Xander's soldiers, including Locheran and Thorne.

I haven't seen much of Thorne ever since he was re-assigned to protect the new vampire queen nearly eight months ago. It's part of a unity plan to eventually reveal supernatural beings to the human world.

Xander's not quite sold on the idea, but next week there's some big supernatural conference being held here in the Big Apple that he has to attend to discuss the serious topic.

So much for a honeymoon, not that we could leave the city.

A gargoyle chaplain leads the ceremony, per gargoyle law, and reads us our vows, which we repeat in front of our witnesses.

"I, Evangeline Bishop-Whethers, promise to love my fated mate and king until the day my heart no longer beats. I will stand by him in sickness and in health. I promise to keep the secrets of his kind. I swear to provide the king with at least one heir, though I wouldn't mind more."

The attendees laugh at that.

"I, Xander Basque, promise to cherish my queen, to love her until the day my heart no longer beats. I will stand by her side in sickness and in health and provide her with all the heirs she desires."

Simple vows, but ones full of love and devotion.

The reception is held inside Xander's penthouse, and we all sip on wine and snack on finger foods. Locheran acts as a DJ, and we dance through the night. My mother left early, and an hour before sunrise, we say our goodbyes to the remaining guests: Locheran and Farrah.

This is only the second time I've seen my bestie in the past year. The first time she visited me was on my forty-first birthday in August. She was uncomfortable the entire night. She refused to make eye contact with Xander, and she kept sneering at Locheran, even with both gargoyles in their model-esque human forms.

I tried asking her what was wrong, but she waved off my concern, blaming exhaustion from work and family drama. We don't talk as much since I moved away. I'm such a horrible friend.

I worried she wouldn't accept the wedding invitation, but she called me, crying with excitement, the moment it arrived in the mail.

"Okay, calling each other king and queen was cute, but what did you mean when you said in your vows that you'll keep the secrets of his kind?" Farrah asks after giving me a hug. She looks stunning tonight. Her fiery red hair falls in chaotic curls around her head. She's wearing a green dress that drapes over her curves like liquid. It has a v-neck that showcases her plentiful cleavage. She's my height, but the pumps she's wearing tonight has her towering over me. "And you said something about fated mates and heirs? I mean, Xander's rich, but that's a weird way to say you plan to have kids. Also, how many can you pop out in your forties?"

She's wasted, and anytime Farrah gets drunk, the filter between her thoughts and mouth disappears.

Aside from the comment about me popping out kids in my forties, I ignore her valid questions and push my friend toward the door.

"You're drunk!" I say with a giggle.

She laughs too. "Guess I am!"

"Locheran!" I yell for my mate's best friend. "Can you walk Farrah to a guest apartment?"

He narrows his eyes at me.

"I am your queen, you know," I say low enough that I know he can hear me, but Farrah can't. "Don't you have to follow my orders?"

He rolls his eyes.

"Yes, Your *Majesty*."

Farrah's cheeks flare red as Locheran approaches, and she quickly looks away. Okay, this is progress. Maybe she doesn't really hate him. Maybe she's intimidated by him. To be fair, Locheran is a cocky asshole sometimes, and he exudes playboy alphahole, especially to people he wants to push away.

I think he's worried I'll kick his ass if he gets involved with Farrah and ends up breaking her heart.

He's right. I would.

I'm still holding out hope that they're fated mates, but Xander says if they were, the connection would have revealed itself by now.

"My lady," he says and holds out his arm.

Farrah lets out a shaky breath and accepts his escort and the two stumble down the hallway to the elevator.

Xander comes up behind me and kisses my neck.

"Hello, *wife.*"

"Hello, *husband.*"

"My queen."

I turn around and stand on my tiptoes to give him a kiss.

"You know," I say when we part, "I've been thinking about the *Kis-meet* app. I don't remember downloading it."

Xander's brows furrow. "Huh, I don't either. I assumed Locheran put it on my phone, but when I asked him, he said no. I thought I was going crazy and maybe downloaded it and forgot."

I push at Xander's chest to lead him to the bedroom. "Maybe it was destiny."

"Then we better not let destiny down."

"Have I told you lately how much I love you?"

Xander beams at me. "No, tell me again."

"Only if you tell me first."

"I love you, I love you, I love you—"

"Okay! I get it," I giggle.

He scoops me up into his arms and we spend our wedding night thanking the mysterious app that paired us together.

The End

Thank You

Did you enjoy Gaga for the Gargoyle? Please consider leaving a review on Amazon, Goodreads, or StoryGraph. Or please share on your social media! Don't be afraid to slide into my DMs (as long as you're not mean)!

Gaga for the Gargoyle is part of the Fated Dates multi-author series and a complete standalone. Want to read more tales of monsters getting matched via phone app? Get the complete series today!

Want more monsters? Check out A Vow for the Vamp and Guardians for the Vamp. Locheran and Farrah's book, Giddy for the Gargoyle, is out now. Get it on Amazon!

Acknowledgements

If you read A Vow for the Vamp, you know why that book was special. I also worked on Gaga for the Gargoyle during recovery following my hysterectomy in March of 2024. There were complications and because of that, my recovery took longer. Then I had a second surgery at the end of June to fix an issue that arose during those complications. Being able to escape to a world of gargoyles helped in my recovery. Because of that, this book will always be one of my favs and I am so grateful to the organizers of the Fated Dates series for letting me be a part of this project.

Let's talk about Evangeline. She's a beautiful plus-size woman in her 40s because that's me! I'm fat & in my 40s! I also wanted a FMC who wasn't newly 18 and had life experience, even if those experiences weren't great.

I want to thank my beta readers: Xan Garcia, Gina Hejtmanek, Mikaelynn Rose, Suzi Vee, and Kara Robinson. Thank you for helping me create this world. I can't wait to write more and get your amazing reactions.

Thank you to my editor Jenny Sliger with Owl Eyes Proofs & Edits. You went ABOVE AND BEYOND for this book and I owe you EVERYTHING.

To my cover artist: Sophie. This cover is perfect. I love Evangeline's little smirk and sexy 'come hither' look. No wonder Xander fell in love at first sight!

And to the readers who have been with me from the beginning and to the ones who just found me, to the readers who buy my books no matter what I release, to the readers who constantly like my posts and share them... I love you all. You mean the world to me and you are the reason I keep writing!

Also by Settle Myer

Guardians for the Vamp

A Manhattan Monsters Romance

FFM with a Vampire/Sphinx/Gargoyle

The monsters of Manhattan are tired of living in the shadows. The new vampire queen, Layla, is tasked to come up with an unveiling plan, but she finds herself distracted by her new broody gargoyle guard... and the bossy sphinx on the unveiling committee. Find it on Amazon & KU.

Gaga for the Gargoyle

A Fated Mates Monster Romance.

Gaga for the Gargoyle is about 999-year-old gargoyle king, Xander, who has 6 months to find his fated mate before permanently turning to stone. Enter a strange dating app that pairs him with Evangeline, a 40-year-old human. This book is part of the Fated Dates series, a shared world about plus-size MCs meeting their monster mates through a mysterious dating app. Find it on Amazon & KU

A Vow for the Vamp

A Manhattan Monsters Romance.

500-year-old vampire queen, Millie, is ready to face the sun, no longer able to live with the guilt of the monster she's become. When she goes out for one last feed, she meets a 29-year-old golden retriever man named Teddy... who just might be the reason she lives. It's on Amazon & KU

Deadly Deceit & Deadly Obsession

Mafia Romance (New York City Syndicate Book 1 & 2) Deadly Deceit is the first book and Deadly Obsession is book 2. Both are standalones. They are dark cozy romance meaning the romance is sweet... but the story includes dark themes. Find them on Amazon & KU

The Off Script Series

Beyond the Bright Lights is the first book in the Off Script series of spicy standalone contemporary romances. It features Lana & Mylan's story. Beyond the Fame is book two and features Rebecca & Jensen's story. Beyond the Spotlight is the third and final book and features Savannah & Reynold's story. Find them on Amazon & KU. Beyond the Bright Lights & Beyond the Fame are on Audible

The Trinity Trilogy

If you love action & adventure, badass women with superpowers, diverse characters, found family, and fated mates—check out my sci-fi romance trilogy. Book 1 is a sweet romance with some cursing and violence, but books 2 & 3 have a sprinkle of spice in them. Trinity Found, Trinity Returns, Trinity Rises. Find them on Amazonand Audible.

About the Author

Settle Myer lives in New York City with her cats Zombie, Michonne & Birdie. She's currently a TV news writer who hopes to one day leave a world of death, disaster, and politics to write about worlds with plenty of cinnamon roll men and badass women. She loves all things zombies, cats, karaoke, and tattoos... but not necessarily in that order.

Social Media

Check out my website and sign up for my newsletter for updates on new books, discounts, and sneak peeks!

https://www.settlemyerauthor.com/

Join my readers group. Become a Settle Myer Star and be a part of the discussion with other fans. I also posts fun facts about my books, characters, and more!

Follow me on social media

tiktok.com/@settlemyerauthor

instagram.com/settlemyerauthor

facebook.com/settlemyerauthor